The Vampire Mechanic

Will Macmillan Jones

First published in 2012 by Safkhet Publishing

Second edition 2014 by Red Kite Publishing Limited

www.redkitepublishing.net

Text Copyright 2013 by Will Macmillan Jones

Find out more about the author on
www.willmacmillanjones.com

Cover Image and Design by Hazel Butler, Aädenian Arts.

www.aadenianarts.com

ISBN-13: 978-1502354730
ISBN-10: 150235473X

DEDICATION

In January 2011 I was lucky enough to find my way to an authors' website. It is basically a big slush pile, where all sorts of authors write all sorts of books, for all sorts of reasons. On there I found a small group of like-minded certifiable lunatics called The Alliance of Worldbuilders. They know who they are. And they were misguided enough to let me in, a decision that I am sure many of them now regret!

If you are interested in reading fantasy, of any type, go and find our website or the Facebook page, both run by The Dark Lord: who like all of the best Dark Lords, remains nameless and faceless. You will find links to some exceptional writers, and exceptional books.

For a writer with any pretensions, these guys are the best friends and internet writing peer group anyone could hope to have. Without their encouragement and help, this series would never have made it out of the dark recesses of my mind and into print.

Great! That means that it's all their fault now, and not mine!
To the guys: The Alliance of Worldbuilders.

CONTENTS

The Cast List   5

1   Chapter One   Pg 7

2   Chapter Two   Pg 24

3   Chapter Three   Pg 29

4   Chapter Four   Pg 50

5   Chapter Five   Pg 57

6   Chapter Six   Pg 71

7   Chapter Seven   Pg 86

8   Chapter Eight   Pg 105

9   Chapter Nine   Pg 115

10 Chapter Ten   Pg 134

11 Chapter Eleven   Pg 148

12 Chapter Twelve   Pg 168

13 Chapter Thirteen   Pg 184

14 Chapter Fourteen   Pg 200

15 Chapter Fifteen   Pg 218

16 Chapter Sixteen   Pg 230

17 Chapter Seventeen   Pg 249

18 Chapter Eighteen   Pg 265

The Cast

The Banned Underground

Fungus	A BogTroll needing the bog(not that bog)
Haemar	A dwarf seeking a high note
Gormless Golem (GG)	A guitarist, who probably has a spare
Scar	Another dwarf, of unsound
Felldyke	A drummer. Poise, timing, chicken
Dai	A drinking dragon
Eddie	A monosyllabic roadie

And look who's back...

The Watches

Ned	Assistant Dark Lord, so under Authority
Ned's assistant, Bill	Authorised to do very little, it seems

And the assistant assistant,

Ben	A taxi driver, so careless of authority

And arriving, as if by accident,

Grizelda	Witch and specialist frog collector
Count Notveryfarout	A leading Vampire, with acute depression

Percival	Possibly the cause of the depression
Hugo	Like buses, Vampires travel in threes

Featured by design of the author (possibly)

Santa's Little Helpers

Mungo	A reluctant accomplice
Jerry	A lover of live music
Fred	Just one of the gang
Boris	There's always one in every gang.

Guilty by association

Notsanta	Turned up, and everyone is too scared to ask him to leave.

And introducing, to thunderous applause

(or more likely, the sound of one hand clapping)

The Vampire Mechanic

Basil	Who blames Christine
And, FREYA	The keyboard just melted

Chapter One

Another day and another gig for the Banned Underground. Only the audience changes: the group members tend to wear the same clothes all the time. The Banned Underground was a mystical Rhythm and Blues band growing rapidly in fame, reputation, and unpaid bar bills. Instead of the normal Dwarf Halls or pubs and clubs (the latter a common haunt of trolls) they had been invited to play a really prestigious gig this time inside The Fairy Hill of North Wales, home to the International Investment Banking Group run by the Edern; a secretive magical race devoted to good works and making stupefyingly enormous sums of money. Not necessarily in that order. But the promised fee was exorbitant, and the hospitality room well stocked. Only the dressing room, as tradition demanded, was dark, with an unsavory aroma. And that was probably the fault of the occupants.

Haemar, lead singer of the Banned Underground (and therefore a dwarf: Fungus the Boogieman, the saxophone playing, luminous green BogTroll was not a dwarf: nor was Dai, the bass player or Eddie The Roadie. The band was only truly prejudiced against rappers) looked around the room, until his glance rested upon Felldyke, the spherical drummer.

Felldyke absentmindedly delved into one of the many specially designed pockets on his smock, and produced a drumstick. He gnawed away at this for a moment, before realising it was wooden, not chicken, and promptly threw it into a corner of the small room in disgust before making an alternative selection from another pocket.

Gormless Golem (aka GG), dwarf guitarist and reformed prog rock aficionado, was nearly invisible: humming something strange to himself with his head buried deep in a cabinet full of electrical stuff no one else could be bothered to understand.

"Just tell us the light show is going to work this time," Fungus implored GG, whilst he cleaned earwax from the reed in his sax.

"Yeah," agreed Scar, the keyboard player. "Last time out, it set my beard on fire."

"That wasn't the light show." GG emerged from the cabinet. "That was Dai, the drunken dragon who was on Bass. * And he's not here this gig."

* [The guitar. Not the beer. Although it could have been both.]

"Tell me why again?" asked Felldyke.

"Because he comes from South Wales. This gig's in North Wales, and he says there's too many RAF jets around. He's fed up of getting shot at."

"They've always missed him so far."

"Yeah, well. He won't come, and that's that."

"We never used to bother with a bass player, anyway," Haemar observed. "We'll get by. Fungus, have you decided on a set list, yet?"

"Well, these are merchant bankers."

"Don't be so rude ter them. They paid us, didn't they?"

"No, they really are merchant bankers, you idiot. So, I thought, how many songs do we know about money?"

"Forget the Pink Floyd one," said GG. "Can't do the effects. And we'd need a bass."

"Have to have *Money Talks*," said Haemar.

"*Wallstreet Shuffle,*" suggested Scar, to approval. He wasn't used to it, and basked in the warmth.

"*Money for Nothing,* " said Felldyke, who was used to hearing the phrase.

"*Take the Money and Run,*" added Haemar, who normally dealt with the promoters.

"*Money Changes Everything,*" suggested Scar, who was a closet Cyndi Lauper fan.

"Have you got an adjustable spanner?" asked Haemar.

"Why?" GG asked.

"Because if you want me ter sing that, I'll need to adjust me underpants so I can reach the high notes."

"OK," Fungus said quickly. "Just the first four, then into the normal set."

"Drinking songs. This lot should be into those too. Scar, have you put that box on the front of the stage yet?" asked Haemar.

"What box?" asked Fungus, perplexed.

"We thought we'd put up a donations box. If they've all had their bonuses, maybe they'll feel generous."

"Generous? This lot? They're bankers. They'd even charge for giving you the time of day."

"Well, you never know. Worth a try."

"Hey, Fungus," asked Scar, " didn't yer invite some mates from the north? Where are they, then?"

"Dunno," said Fungus. Worry and concern failed to spread across his face. "Maybe they had transport problems."

"Come on," called Haemar from the door. " I think they're ready for us."

✳

Two thousand feet over the Irish Sea, Fungus' friends were indeed having some transport troubles.

"I told you we should have taken the car instead," whined Mungo.*

*[There's always one who has to have known better, isn't there?]

"Well we didn't, so shut up," replied Jerry, who was steering.

"Does any one actually know where we are?" Mungo grumbled.

"Fred's navigating," grunted Jerry, peering through the clouds. Unfortunately, his view was impeded by their power source. A glance at the controls on the dashboard showed him very little.

"Fred?"

"Sorry," grumbled Fred. "I was relying on the SatNav, and all it will tell me is that it's lost."

"Like us then," grunted Jerry, ducking back behind the windshield.

"Haven't you got a map?" asked Mungo.

"Course!" Fred snapped back. "But for that to do any good, we need to see the ground first, to get a fix on our position."

"I saw the ground a moment ago," contributed Boris.

"And?" three faces looked at him expectantly.

"I saw the sea."

"Oh very helpful. Look, there's only forty minutes until the gig starts. Anyone got any ideas?"

"My phone's started working!" crowed Boris. "It's got a SatNav on it too. And a compass."

"Try it quick," said Jerry. "I'll lose a bit of height, see if that helps."

"Maps have come up," said Boris, excitedly. "We're not far from Anglesey, we can be there in twenty minutes!"

Jerry and Fred looked at each other slowly. "Anglesey? Oh dear."

On Anglesey, the ever-watchful, unsleeping eye of the evening shift Controller working for the UK Air Defense System blinked rapidly: he stroked his moustache, and raised his second cup of tea of the shift towards his lips: only to spray the refreshing liquid across the screen and console in front of him as the computer alerts started flashing urgent signals. Grabbing the microphone with one hand, he sounded the General Alert with the other.

"Unidentified incoming, moving fast towards the coast!" he yelled at his colleagues, and operated the headset that provided his hotline to the standby interceptors.

"Victor Kilo One Six, Scramble. This is not a drill, repeat this is not a drill."

"Victor Kilo One Six, airborne from Valley airfield," replied the interceptor pilot, as his Hawk jet fighter left the ground in a fury of noise from the afterburner.

"Victor Kilo One Six, Valley Controller. Intruder bearing 030 degrees. Height 1500 feet, inbound, moving fast."

"Valley Controller, Victor Kilo. Have radar contact, arming missiles. Should be visual on the target at any moment..."

"Victor Kilo, Valley Controller. Radar Traces merged. Are you visual on target?"

"Valley, Victor Kilo One Six. Negative, too much cloud to see. Wait... It's Santa's Sleigh being pulled by two reindeer! They've taken evading action!!"

"Victor Kilo One Six, Valley Controller. Disarm missiles, return to base at once. Confirm instructions!"

"I dunno," muttered the Controller to his colleague. "Last year he saw dragons, this year Santa Claus. And it's not even Christmas."

"Told you we were near Anglesey!" yelled Boris, who had almost fallen out of The Sleigh at the wild dive, and was struggling to climb back in.

"He'll never find us again in this cloud," shouted back Jerry, increasing their speed.

"If Himself finds out we've been seen, there'll be hell to pay," worried Mungo.

"Look, we'll see the gig and get back home before He gets back from that cruise He's gone on. Stop moaning," Jerry ordered.

"Is that the coast ahead?"

"Looks like it. Now, head South, with a touch of West."

"You sure?"

"Down this valley, to the end."

The Sleigh flew on in silence. Except for the occasional interruptions from the reindeer, who were fed up because they hadn't been fed up before flying.

"Bunsen and Burner are getting fed up," warned Mungo.

"Not far to go now," Jerry insisted.

"Come on, they'll be on soon," grumbled Fred.

"Fungus is always late on stage."

"Yeah, but this gig's for the Edern, and they are sticklers for protocol. Always have their stockings at the same angle on the mantelpieces."

"How come you got tickets, anyway?" asked Boris.

"Mungo and I did Fungus a favour last year, when he was in a spot of bother. We couldn't get to his last gig, so he sent me tickets for this one."

"Which we are going to miss. WHOOOOOOO! Watch that hill!" yelled Boris.

"Missed it, didn't I?"

BOOOIIINNNNNGGGGGGGG

"Didn't miss that one Jerry, did you?"

"Look, Jerry, you've left damn great tracks across the hillside back there!"

"You ought to go back later, and fill them in, you know," worried Fred.

"Sorry guys. But look, the reindeer are getting tired now. Normally there's six of them on The Sleigh, not two."

"Can't we climb?" asked Boris.

"We can. The 'deer can't," Jerry advised him.

Bunsen made a loud (and disgusting) noise. The Sleigh lost a bit more height.

"Maybe if we lose some weight?" suggested Fred, looking wildly around the interior.

"I've already lost a bit when we nearly hit that fighter jet," moaned Mungo.

Ahead loomed a large hill, a very large hill, in fact a small mountain. The reindeer did their best.

The concert hall in the heart of the Fairy Hill was full of exited and enthusiastic Edern, sat at the various tables scattered around the hall. They had put up with the catering disaster that is traditional at Company Dinners, and were now hoping for something better.

The compere for the night was one of the senior executives, tall and patrician looking, whose dress had cost enough to clear the financial deficit of a small country. The noise from the crowd was subdued, but appreciative as Lady Hankey walked out onto the stage, and waved for quiet. Just when even someone with impaired hearing could have heard a pin drop, Felldyke dropped... a cymbal.*

* [Surely you were not thinking of something else? Shame on you!]

Fungus stuck his head out between the curtains that concealed their preparations. "Sorry!" he called, adjusted his sunglasses and vanished.

Lady Hankey opened her mouth again, only to be drowned out by the sound of Haemar gargling to moisten his throat. Sniggers ran around the room, possibly they were too nervous to stop and be identified.

"Sorry!" called Haemar, behind the curtain.

With an effort, Lady Hankey tried again "Our very own CEO, Lord Blear," she paused and received the benefit of polite applause, before continuing: "has authorised the use of his very own Company Expense Account to arrange for the (tax deductible) entertainment we are about to enjoy. He cannot be here in person, being involved in some high level negotiations at the Treasury Department, where he hopes to have our Fairy Hill Headquarters designated an International Tax-Free Haven, on account of our non-relative time banding zone."

Another murmur of more enthusiastic applause followed.

"And so tonight, it falls to me to introduce, fresh," (behind the curtain, GG sniffed pointedly and glared at Felldyke) "from their triumph somewhere small and insignificant, THE BANNED UNDERGROUND!"

Louder applause greeted this last announcement, and Lady Hankey quickly vacated the stage as the curtains were flung back, and Haemar strutted to the front of the stage, his mike in one hand and his scarf (soaked in best bitter) in the other.

"Here we go!" he yelled, and the Banned launched into their traditional opening number, *Going Underground.*

Two more numbers, and the crowd were dancing. As GG played out *Money for Nothing,* Haemar stepped back to the mike.

"We've tailored this part of the set to celebrate your Investment Banking Successes of the year," he growled. The assembled Edern failed to cheer as the Banned took a deep breath and ripped into *Easy Living.*

"I say!" Lady Hankey observed to her companion, "that Fungus has a dry sense of humour."

"Must be why he keeps pouring that bottle down his throat then. Lubrication."

Fortunately, GG chose that moment to crank up the volume on Scar's keyboard until the sound was deafening.

"Why have you messed with the mix?" Haemar yelled into GG's ear.

"Hides his bum notes!" GG yelled back.

"I can see that."

"He can't!"

"That's because he always plays with his eyes shut...."

Both ducked as Felldyke lost his grip on another drumstick, which flew across the stage into the audience. The lucky banker who grabbed it in mid flight (before it landed in his left eye) sulked to see it was unsigned.

"What's next?" GG asked Fungus, who was already short of breath.

"*Money Talks*. Then we'll take a break."

"You've only gone and broken it!" accused Mungo, as he fussed around the two disgruntled reindeer.

Jerry and Fred climbed out of The Sleigh, and walked back along their track for a short distance. Then they each grabbed hold of a large boot sticking out of the peat bog, and pulled as hard as they could until a somewhat dishevelled Boris appeared.

"Thanks fellers," he gasped.

Fred looked around in the gloom, as they meandered back to The Sleigh.

"Where are we?" he asked.

"Allt y Cnicht," said Jerry.

"Bless you."

"No, that's the name of the hill." Jerry lowered his voice. "They say that anyone who spends a night here comes down either a poet or a madman in the morning."

"You've been here before then," said Mungo, still soothing the reindeer.

"But I'm no good at poems."

The others all looked at Jerry without speaking. Mungo shook his head.

"How bad is it?"

"What?" answered Boris.

"The Sleigh, of course!"

They all looked at The Sleigh. Even the most technically inept could see that it wasn't going to fly again without major reconstructive surgery.

"We are going to have to leave it here," said Jerry, nervously.

"What, in full view of the Customers?" objected Mungo.

"Got any better ideas?"

"I've got an idea," said Boris.

"Bet it's lonely, then."

"Oh, very funny. That one's older than the reindeer."

"Go on then," encouraged Jerry. "Tell us."

"We leave The Sleigh, and go to the gig on the reindeer."

"And then?"

"Simple. When the gig has finished, we get Fungus and his roadie to collect The Sleigh, and tow it to that mechanic Himself uses. His garage is not that far from here. We get it fixed, bribe the mechanic to keep his mouth shut, and go home before He gets back."

Silence greeted this.

"Well, lads?"

"I never knew you had it in you," said Fred, slowly.

"Brilliant!" raved Jerry.

As one, the four Santa's Little Helpers turned to look at the reindeer, who looked back at them with deep suspicion. Ten minutes later, the overloaded reindeer cantered into the car park at Fairy Hill. Security had tried to stop them at the gate, but no one can stop His reindeer when they are on a mission, so squashing objections (and the guards) had been easy.

"Just in time for the second half!" shouted Jerry, leading the charge into the hall.

Without the aid of the curtain, the Banned were regrouping for the second half of the set.

"Start with *Red, Red Wine*," suggested Haemar.

"We're meant to be playin', not putting in orders at the bar," objected Felldyke.

"*Four To The b*ar then," said GG.

"'Cos there's only four of us at this gig?"

"Because it's a good song."

"Hey look!" cried Fungus, who for once had abstained from the discussion.

"At what?" asked his friends, whose minds were as suspicious as Elvis'.

"My mates have arrived. Look, there at the back of the hall."

The Banned looked, somewhat blearily for the hospitality room had indeed been well stocked. At the back of the room were four very tall, rather dishevelled characters of a vaguely elvish appearance, who were arguing with security.

"Of course we're with the Banned. Look, we've got these t-shirts on."

"Their roadie's been selling those at the gate. Could have bought them there," answered an unimpressed guard, whose attitude had been coloured by his inability to get to the bar during the interval. Jerry bent down, and whispered something in his ear. The guard stiffened, and then went white and backed away hurriedly, allowing all four into the hall.

"Don't we know them?" asked GG as the four, much taller than the Edern all around them, headed for the bar.

"Santa's Little Helpers," answered Fungus.

"Little? There's not one of them under six foot six!"

"It's only a job description. They helped us out the last time we were in Wales, so I sent them some tickets as a thank you."

"Fair enough," shrugged Haemar, who wasn't interested enough to remember.

At the back of the Concert hall, the Security Guard shook himself, and assumed a stern countenance as a medium sized lady approached him, with a view to gaining admittance.

"I'm sorry madam: No ticket, no admittance!" The guard began to slam the door, and then found his newly acquired status as an amphibian a hindrance.

"Rivet! Rivet!! Rivet!!!" he complained.

"It's only temp'ry," reassured the lady, carefully stepping over the frog.

On stage, with little forward planning, the Banned swung into action for the second half of the set.

"Hey, they're really good!" Mungo was finally enjoying himself.

Boris was dancing to *Shaking All Over* with an aristocratic Edern lady. Fred was lying across the bar, swapping drinks and rude jokes with a dwarf of his acquaintance, leaving just Jerry for Mungo to talk to.

"Yeah, they're not a bad band at all," Jerry shouted back. He looked confused as two frogs hopped disconsolately past on the bar top.

"What did you say to that security guard at the door?" asked Mungo.

"I reminded him what Himself put in the guard's stocking on the last Round."

"What was it?"

Jerry looked around, and bent close to Mungo's ear before telling him. Mungo looked very shocked, then burst out into hysterical laughter, in a nice counterpoint to Haemar's vocals.

"He wouldn't want *that* to get around!"

They turned back to the bar, where the bartender was refusing to serve three frogs. Boris joined them.

"I thought you were well in with her you were dancing with?" asked Mungo.

"It's Fungus' fault," said Boris, gloomily.

"How can it be his fault?" asked Jerry. "He's onstage!"

"I know. But I was doing Ok, until they started playing *Please Don't Touch* and that gave her an excuse to get away."

Mungo was shaking too much with laughter to comment, so Jerry gave Boris a beer. Onstage the Banned started on *Jailhouse Rock* as the set drew towards an end.

"Prophetic," mused Boris.

"What do you mean?" asked Mungo, who had now calmed down a bit.

"Himself will put us in the jailhouse if we don't get The Sleigh sorted."

"Can you remember what the mechanic is called?" asked Jerry.

"Idiot," said Boris.

"Oi, there's no need for that. I asked a civil enough question."

"No, Himself always calls the mechanic 'Idiot'."

"Oh, I see. Well, he must have another name."

"Basil," came a voice from behind them.

They turned, slowly, to see a medium sized, middle aged lady of pleasant appearance.*

*[Which proves how deceptive appearances can be. And if *she* asks, the editor wrote that, not me.]

On the bar, now behind them, the frogs started moving away very quickly.

"I'm sorry for buttin' in, but I overheard yer conversation on my way to the bar. The lad you want is called Basil."

"How do you know him, madam?" asked Jerry, politely.

"He came ter me for some help earlier this year. You see, he'd been turned into a vampire a few years back."

Mungo was not surprised. "I've seen the bills for his work. I thought he'd been one for years."

"Apparently not. Anyway, you know how mechanics always suck their teeth? When they're planning a way to double the bill? Well that's a problem fer a vampire."

Jerry nodded. "We've met him before."

"Well, I were helping him with his problem."

Santa's Little Helpers shuddered.

"Thank you so much. You didn't tell us your name, madam?" asked Mungo.

"I'm Grizelda, witch of the Third Pentangle."

"Thank you again. If there is anything we can do in return?"

"Yes, there is," said Grizelda.

"Uh?"

"Shift out of me way, so as I can get ter the bar before the second half of the set finishes."

"Oh. Right. Sorry."

The Little Helpers scattered as Grizelda made her way to the bar, and smiled sweetly at the bartender. Who ducked.

Chapter Two

The Edern had clearly reached the end of their party. Assorted bodies were strewn around the hall, showing all the signs of being intoxicated by the music, the dancing, and the small amount of alcohol Lord Blear had authorised. And the substantially larger amounts of alcohol, which the bartender had authorised. As the Banned Underground reached the end of their set, a storming version of *Johnny B Goode*, which would have roused the dead but failed with the drunken Edern, Jerry led his little troop backstage.

Security stopped them.

"Sorry, probably Sirs. No entry."

"I've got backstage passes," said Jerry, showing them to the guard.

"I can't read. Have to do better then that."

Mungo leant forward and whispered in the guard's ear.

The guard was unmoved. "All me family got one of those."

Mungo looked alarmed. "I'm glad I wasn't at your house at Christmas then."

The immediate threat of violence was removed (as was the guard) when Fungus opened the backstage door and knocked the guard off the stage.

"Hiya, guys!" he said. " Cool you could make it to the gig. Come in and meet the boys."

Jerry led his friends into the backstage area. Fuelled by their reading of books about the after gig antics of The Faces, The Rolling Stones, Led Zeppelin and others, they were expecting a wild debauched scene. Felldyke pandered to their preconceptions by lying on the floor with a drumstick (chicken) stuffed up each nostril, another in one ear and two in his mouth. Scar lay on his back on a couch, with his mouth open. He steadily poured liquid from a can into the orifice. GG was fussing with some electrics, and Haemar was gargling again, although this time with a bottle of whisky. An open, empty red box lay at his feet.

"Hey Guys!" shouted Fungus. "Me mates are here."

There was a general muted chorus of hellos, and general indifference. Fungus led his friends over to the drinks table, and started them on the buffet. Mungo moved politely to one side, and his foot accidentally brushed a heavy bag tied to one end of the table. He froze as three swords instantaneously appeared at his neck.

"Don't go near the bag," growled Haemar, relaxing.

"What's in it?" asked Mungo.

"Don't ask."

"Sorry." The swords were slowly withdrawn, and the bag miraculously vanished, to reappear a moment later tied to Felldyke's leg.

"How was your trip?" asked Fungus.

"Ah. Bit of a problem, I was going to ask for your help there," answered Jerry.

Fungus looked alarmed.

"Why?"

"Well, we sort of had a crash," started Jerry.

"In The Sleigh," added Mungo.

"And we could do with a bit of help to get it to Basil, the mechanic."

"Oh, we can probably help out there, lads," said Fungus, still convivial from the gig. The noises from the rest of the Banned were less encouraging.

"Every time that sort of thing happens, we get into trouble," objected Scar.

"I'm fed up of prisons," agreed GG.

"You haven't played any prog rock in ages, so you should be all right," replied Fungus, referring to his guitarist's original crime (for which he had been rightfully imprisoned.)

The door opened again.

"Rivet, rivet" complained Security. The room grew very still, very quickly.

"Hello you lot. Good gig," said Grizelda, sweetly.

Haemar tried to hide inside his helmet. GG dived headfirst into the speaker stack for safety and Scar hid behind Felldyke who, tied to the takings, couldn't move.

"Hello Grizelda," said Fungus, meekly. Santa's Little Helpers tried to hide behind Fungus, but as there were four of them, each a foot taller than Fungus, their efforts were unsuccessful.

Grizelda glared around the room. "Own up who left those reindeer in the car park. They tried to eat my goat." Her slightly smug expression showed that Bunsen and Burner had failed in this objective.

"What happened then?" asked Haemar cautiously.

"Oh they made friends. Eventually. I left them having a competition about who could fart the loudest. But it were antisocial to leave them there in the first place. They could have got hurt."

Jerry, who had a long acquaintance with the reindeer, doubted that. But wisely didn't say so.

"What are you planning to do with them?" demanded Grizelda.

"Eerrr" replied Jerry.

"Typical. No idea eh? Well, they can come back with me and the goat fer a bit.

Fred's face lit up. He didn't like the reindeer very much either.

"How did you know about all this?" Fungus asked Grizelda, carefully.

"I overheard this lot in the bar asking about Basil, Santa's mechanic. So, are you lot going to help them get it fixed then? You still have that trailer yer borrowed off me."

"How come you're here, anyway? Thought you were in South Wales." Haemar asked her.

"I've been stopping not far from here on a contract job."

No one felt inclined to question her further. They might have had an answer.

"Where's Eddie?" asked GG, still hidden inside a speaker.

Eddie was the Banned's roadie, and general factotum. (A superior name for a gofer.) He had been a professional taxi driver, until a combination of unusual circumstances and a powerful punch on the jaw (from Grizelda's sister) had encouraged a career change, and a speech impediment.

"Outside at yer van," Grizelda told him. There was a silence.

"Right then, now that that's all settled, I'll just take the reindeer back with me until yer need them," said Grizelda.

Boris started to protest, but the other three very quickly shut him up. Grizelda's reputation, and her skill with the people/frog spell had travelled widely. Unlike her laundry. The door swung shut behind Grizelda as she left and the Banned relaxed. Apart from GG who found it hard to relax upside down inside a speaker stack. "Get Eddie!" he called in a muffled sort of way. "And no one touch the guitar!

"The Telecaster?" asked Haemar innocently, reaching out for the guitar still plugged into the amp...plugged into the speaker...

The feedback drowned the agonised howls.

Chapter Three.

Meanwhile, (as they say in all the best books and so inevitably included here) the crash of The Sleigh had not gone unnoticed. The Senior Partner in a certain accounting firm called

TGM ACCOUNTANTS AND TAX CONSULTANTS

had also become acquainted with the matter. When Ned, the Senior Taxation manager, entered the inner sanctum of his employer he found said employer peering urgently into a computer screen whilst his dragon faced (and dragon bodied on a Saturday night) receptionist pointed one talon at something displayed on the screen.

The Senior Partner, as befitted his status, had a big desk, bad breath and a worse attitude. He was also the leader of the local Dark Coven, and went by the name of The Grey Mage. (Or Sir to his friends, who were few in number.)

"Ah, Ned," said The Grey Mage. "You're here."

"Yes Boss. You sent fer me."

"I know I sent for you. That's why you're here."

"Everyone's got ter be somewhere."

"True, Ned. But that does not normally include my office. Pull up that chair, I have a mission for you."

"Good. I was getting bored doing bad tax returns."

"Well, now you can do some goods returned instead. I need you to go to North Wales."

Inside his pinstriped suit, Ned twitched. The words evoked bad memories.

"Take your junior. And that idiot taxi driver, too, as transport."

Ned twitched more violently this time. Evil memories flickered across his consciousness, like an early Hammer House of Horror movie.

"You will need some disguises again."

"Can't we go in normal gear this time, boss?"

"Hum. Travel looking like accountants. That might fool them."

"Who?"

"That Fungus and his dwarf band."

"Nah. They won't get fooled again."

"All right, then I'll save the money. Use your own kit."

"We'll need expenses."

The Grey Mage pushed, reluctantly, a credit card across the desk, and Ned cheered up a bit.

"That'll do nicely," he said.

"It's only for essentials," warned The Grey Mage.

Ned made a private mental list of essentials, which appeared to differ materially from the mental list his boss had envisaged, and so earned him a prescient glare.

"Just because I am sending those two idiots with you doesn't mean you can spend all the time in the pub," The Grey Mage warned.

"We're following Fungus the Boogieman and his band. They spend as much time in the pub as they can. How else do we follow them?"

"Sit in the car park. You can make one drink last all night," scowled The Grey Mage.

Ned's look of acquiescence fooled no one in the room.

Gloria, the Grey Mage's secretary scraped her talon down the computer screen, making the two men wince. Ned (for he was not yet a fully qualified accountant) at the noise, and his boss (who was) at the probable cost.

"Look at the screen" she said, before turning her attention to the rapidly diminishing supply of chocolate biscuits, one open clue to her dragon nature.*

* [Dragons might be able to conceal their wings behind a smart suit, avoid casually incinerating policemen and traffic wardens by wearing sunglasses, but cannot overcome their desire for a chocolate digestive. Or ten.]

Gloria wandered over to the sideboard, and pulling the stopper out of the traditional whisky decanter (kept to impress clients with the accountant's convivial spirit) took a sniff. Recoiling, she hammered the top back in as fast as she could, in the cause of Health and Safety.

"Have you ever given this stuff to a client?" she demanded.

"George, from that needle manufacturer we used to have," confessed her employer.

"The one that died in mysterious circumstances?" Gloria asked.

"They weren't mysterious," put in Ned. " He fell, climbing out of his neighbour's bedroom window."

"When his neighbour came home unexpectedly to have lunch with his wife," added the Grey Mage.

"So, not because he'd drunk this excuse for a malt?" the secretary looked unconvinced.

"Apparently not."

"Well, it should have been. Now, I'm going back to the front desk." The secretary flounced, as only a dragon in disguise can, out of the room.

The Grey Mage scowled after her, and made a mystical sign in the air. "Look what she's done to my packet of biscuits!" he complained, before screwing the empty wrapper up and dropping into an otherwise empty drawer on his filing cabinet marked 'Practice Accounts-Confidential'.

"Just as well she didn't see the real whisky you keep in the bottom drawer of yer desk, then," commented Ned.

His boss gave him a steely glare, wondering if his managerial staff all knew what else was kept there. (They did.)

"Right," he instructed. "Look at this on the screen."

"The big scratch?"

"No, dummy, the picture."

"Is that that Norad website, Boss? The Air Defense North America computer system?"

"Yes, Ned, it is. The one that tracks Santa's progress around the world."

"I thought that they only ran that computer once a year. The rest of the time they only use it to order the pizza and watch reruns of Friends."

"Wrong. Well, you are right, actually. But it *is* set to run automatically when Event Triggered."

"What's the Event, Boss?"

"It's actually programmed to pick up The Sleigh. We are used to seeing it every year on The Round, but Himself also takes it out a couple of times during the year. Training runs for the Reindeer, and an annual service. This is neither of those. It is unplanned, and unexplained."

"And uninteresting," muttered Ned.

"Ned, it has been a target of our Dark Wizard Coven for some years to acquire The Sleigh. And my old Mercedes is clapped out. I fancy The Sleigh as a change."

"Will that be a good swap, Boss? Your old Mercedes has been around the world a few times, but not as often as Santa's Sleigh."

"Many benefits will come to he who captures The Sleigh. Advancement in The Order, and accelerated passes for your Tax Institute exams, your own space in the car park."

"We don't have a car park at the office, though. I have ter leave my car at the supermarket and walk."

"Well I'm sending the three of you out to capture The Sleigh. For the glory of the Dark Order of Caer Surdin."

"And what else?" demanded Ned, unconvinced.

"Well, there is a big reward offered as well. You, as Team Leader will of course be well rewarded."

"Ah, now I'm motivated. Where is it, then?"

"In Wales."

Ned twitched again.

"Are you all right?" asked The Grey Mage.

"Yes Boss. Just, why is it always Wales?"

"The author lives there, I'm told. Lazy beggar can't be bothered to drive round looking for new locations."

"Typical," grumbled Ned.

"Anyway, this one isn't one of Santa's regular trips. So, He probably doesn't know The Sleigh's in trouble."

"How do we know?"

"Well, the computer is set to monitor Norad's tracking of The Sleigh, and the alarm went off an hour ago. We've extrapolated from the data to calculate a likely destination based on available parameters."

"Say again?" asked Ned.

"Our Coven leader made an educated guess. The track The Sleigh will take leads directly to the Fairy Hill of the Edern. Who, we know, have booked a certain band for a gig there tonight."

"Which is where The Banned come into it."

"Yes. So, your mission is:"

"I can guess. Go ter Wales. Steal The Sleigh. Return here with it."

"And you will be richly rewarded," responded The Grey Mage with a straight face.

Ned had some reservations at this point, but kept them to himself.

"Your able and willing assistants," (it was a tribute to the professional accounting skills of The Grey Mage that he was able to say that with a straight face) "are waiting in reception for you." The Grey Mage pointed to the door of his office, and Ned headed that way. As he reached the door, his employer spoke again.

"You messed up last year over the Throne of the Mountain King. This time, be successful."

Ned paused, thought of a number of rude retorts, and decided against them.

Opening the office door, (and carefully closing it behind himself), he looked around reception. His two assistants were sitting quite still in the uncomfortable chairs reserved for official visitors from the tax office, and were kept warm by the roasting glare of the dragon receptionist.

"Get yer kit, meet me in the car park in an hour." Ned instructed them.

"Where we off to this time?" asked the junior assistant.

"Tell you in the car."

"Bet it's going ter be Wales again," said the assistant assistant, with foreboding.

"What makes yer think that?"

"My SatNav refused to turn on this morning on the way ter work."

"What were yer bothering with it for anyway? You only live around the corner. Even you couldn't get lost round here."

"Well, last week I put that new thing on it" said the assistant assistant.

"What new thing?"

"Prescient Predictive Progression it's called."

"So what is it then?"

"Well, it's supposed to predict fer itself where you are going ter be going, and work all the routes out for you in advance."

"Does it work?"

"Suppose so. It worked out where we were going ter be told to go, and sulked about it all day."

"Well, any road," Ned put his foot down, "get your stuff ready. We've got a big mission this time."

Two hours later, all three met in the car park, and climbed into the elderly taxi that did duty as the Dark Coven's eldritch transport.

"So, where are we off to?" asked the driver, trying again to activate the SatNav.

Ned leant forward, and his hand passed over the screen, which lit up.

"How did you manage that?" asked the junior, impressed.

"Were it a mystic pass?" asked the assistant assistant, also impressed.

"No. I tweaked the power cable. It was loose." Ned told them.

"Amazing. So, where are we goin?" asked Ned's junior.

"Wales."

"I knew it," objected the SatNav.

"Trawsfynydd."

"Excuse you."

"What?"

"Didn't you sneeze?"

"The place name is Trawsfynydd," said Ned checking his notes.

"If you insist," sulked the SatNav.

"Just set the route," growled Ned.

"Head for the motorway, and turn North," instructed the SatNav.

"NORTH I SAID!" yelled the SatNav a few minutes later.

"We heard you. But we all know that we have to go south from here."

The SatNav set up a barrage of complaints. Ned pulled the power cable out of the socket, and the complaints turned to abuse and slowly faded away. The elderly *Mondeo* made its arthritic way South past Manchester, and then headed West. Ned had pulled out a map that appeared to be as old as the car, and was (for want of a better word) navigating. "I'm looking fer the A 55 road. But it's not on this map."

The junior assistant leant forward, and peered over his shoulder. "Yes it is."

"Where?"

"Under that chocolate stain."

"Are you sure?"

A huge blast on an air horn from the lorry overtaking them suggested that the other road users did not appreciate the active participation of the driver in the examination of the chocolate stain.

The junior assistant wound down his window, and shouted something. One of the back wheels on the lorry promptly exploded and caught fire, causing the driver to brake wildly. The *Mondeo* accelerated past the stricken lorry, with the junior looking smug in the back.

"Nice," acknowledged Ned. "But next time, ask me first. I'm Team Leader, and it's my job to do that."

"You always hog all the fun though."

"That's because I'm Team Leader."

"Do I take this exit?" asked the assistant assistant.

"Good Grief, no! That way's Liverpool. How much trouble do yer want ter get into?"

"I get all me car spares from Liverpool. Cheap, they are, too."

"And where do yer think *they* get them from? Drive this car into the 'pool, we'd walk out the other side."

"Crane you would need," muttered Ned's junior.

"What are yer on about?" demanded Ned.

"When Keith Moon drove into the pool, they needed a crane to get his car out. Saw a picture of it."

"Turn left," ordered Ned.

"Doesn't he sound like the SatNav?" asked the assistant assistant.

"Just aim for Mold." Ned instructed, looking at the map.

"There's no mould on the car. Cleaned it before we came out."

"Why did I get you two? What's on the CD?"

"*Are Friends Electric.*"

"Well, they can be shocking. Drive faster."

"Sorry, oh Team Leader. Until the Boss buys us new wheels, this is as fast as it gets."

"Forty nine miles an hour?"

"Well, we are downwind," said the assistant assistant.

"Good job, Ned. He was on the curry last night. His wind's awful," the junior said.

The taxi turned onto the A 494, and Ned put the power lead back into the SatNav. The screen turned bright red, and then slowly settled down as green words flashed across too quickly for the eye to read

"What were all them words for then?" Ned asked.

"That's the disclaimer. Stops you setting lawyers on the makers if you get lost using the functions. Course, I usually get lost trying to make it work at all," explained the driver.

"And if you manage it yer always get lost as well," came a voice from the back seat.

"Get Lost," muttered the driver.

"Engaging 'Lost' function," remarked the SatNav helpfully.

"Oh now look what you clowns have done!" screamed the assistant assistant.

"What?"

"It's going ter get us lost!"

"But it always does that anyway. What's the difference?"

"This time it will do it on purpose!"

"Then maybe, just maybe, it will drop us where we want to be instead then?" theorized Ned.

"More likely drop us deep in it," worried the assistant assistant.

"Where are we?" demanded the SatNav.

The three Dark Wizards exchanged perplexed glances.

"You've got the GPS, you tell us," suggested the assistant assistant, cautiously.

Next moment, the SatNav uttered an unearthly wail of pain reminiscent of a Black Sabbath vocal. "You've brought us to Wales," it wailed.

"Oh shut up," Ned told it. "Now, you know where I want us ter go."

"Do I, clever clogs?" asked the SatNav.

"Yes. Because of that PPP thing."

"It's all a load of P," muttered the junior, from the back seat.

"I suppose you want the Fairy Hill Investment Group, then," offered the SatNav.

"Got it," said Ned, his brain working furiously.

"It's not easy, that place. They've put all sorts of magical wards up to keep visitors away, ever since that Tax Inspector managed to blag his way in a few years ago, pretending to be from the electricity company fault team."

"What happened to him?" asked the junior.

"He got away twelve months later, claimed 10 years worth of back pay on personal elapsed time and bought a casino in Monaco. But they don't want to let any more in."

"Well, we're not Tax inspectors. We're accountants," stated Ned.

"If you'd said auditors you'd have had no chance. I'm pre-programmed to self destruct at that."

The three wizards looked at each other.

"Shouldn't have said that, should I?" asked the SatNav, with a worried tone.

Ned smiled. Although he clearly needed the practice, the SatNav got the hint very quickly.

"Route coming up, Sir. Straight ahead for half an hour."

Ned sat back, looking satisfied. "What's next on that CD?" he asked.

"*Paranoid.*"

"Typical," said the SatNav, sotto voice.

The taxi drove on with little conversation for some time. The passengers examined the scenery with interest, whilst the driver was bemused by several of the road signs.

"That one says 'Araf'"* pointed out the driver.

41

*[*Welsh word meaning: 'Slow Down'. This is a traffic warning for tourists, and so not printed in English.]

"Well, do what it tells you then," said the Team Leader.

"Yeah," came a voice from the back seat. "Last year you didn't, and we wound up spending the beer money getting some farmer to tow us out of his field."

"But I still haven't worked out what it means. Look, that one says 'Arafwch.'"

"I didn't hear it say anything."

"Probably because the CD is too loud," complained the assistant assistant.

"*Crash*, by the Primitives. Got to play it loud."

"Prescient Prediction Path complete," remarked the SatNav. The driver turned to look at it.

The taxi, failing to araf as instructed, also failed to take the next corner and drove straight into a field. Via the hedge. And a ditch. And so crashed.

"Now look what you made me do," complained the assistant assistant, who had also become a backseat driver. Whilst holding the steering wheel.

Ned climbed out of what had once been a proud product of the Ford factory, and examined the remains. "I don't think it's going much further," he said.

The others also climbed out, in the case of the assistant assistant by the window, as the door was disinclined to open.

"How far to the Fairy Hill?" asked the junior.

"About five minutes walk," replied Ned. He reached into what had been a car, and pulled out a small briefcase.

"We can't leave it there," protested the assistant assistant. "What if someone finds it and drives off in it?"

The junior examined the wreckage critically. "Nobody's ever going ter drive that anywhere ever again," he commented.

"But that's me living!" worried the assistant assistant.

"It were nearly you're dying too. So be grateful for small mercies."

"Small mercy is what the wife will show me when she finds out," complained the assistant assistant.

"Look," said Ned, " it died on active service. When we get back, the boss will get you another." He reached into the cabin, and pulled out the SatNav.

"What's going on?" the SatNav enquired, urgently.

"Your owner has killed the car, and stranded us," said the junior, with a touch of malice in his voice.

"Stranded us. *In Wales?*" screamed the SatNav.

"Stop panicking. We know where we can get a drink before dark."

"Don't care about that." The SatNav's voice dropped an octave. "They still have druids here."

"Get off," scoffed the junior.

"Straight up. And druids like to capture us and use us in their obscene rituals."

"How obscene?" asked the assistant assistant and the junior

assistant together.

"Dreadful. You wouldn't want to know."

"Oh yes we would," they assured the SatNav, for once united.

"Trust me, you wouldn't."

"Trust us, we do."

"Well, if you must know, when the Druids capture a SatNav, they tie it to the altar stone of their great circles, and if sunrise is not spot on the prediction, they ritually sacrifice us with a dirty great hammer, then melt the remnants. Obscene, see."

The three Dark Wizards looked at each other. Far from being obscene, this seemed like reasonable, rational behaviour to them.

"Why don't they just buy one on eBay like everyone else, rather than capture them?" asked Ned, intrigued.

"Spoils the thrill of the chase, I expect," suggested the assistant assistant.

"No. The Druids were banned by the Romans, so they aren't eligible for any grants from the Government, you see. So they don't have much funding to buy stuff for their rituals," the SatNav explained.

"How do they manage then?" asked Ned.

"Donations from the public, I suppose."

"Donating SatNavs? I could see that," said the assistant assistant.

"Which way now?" asked the junior.

"Turn Left!" yelled the SatNav, its voice fading as Ned dropped it into his pocket.

The three wizards reached the field gate, and turned right.

"What about the car?" asked the junior. "We don't want to leave any traces"

"It were my car, not Tracy's", objected the assistant assistant.

They ignored him.

"You're right," agreed Ned. "We'll burn it."

"You can't do that," objected the assistant assistant. "This isn't Liverpool. Someone will notice."

Ned muttered something under his breath, and waved vaguely at the remains of the taxi, which promptly burst into flames. They walked off down the road, with the car blazing at their backs and the SatNav blazing in Ned's pocket. The driver tossed a steering wheel he just happened to be carrying into the hedge. Before long, the eldritch shape of the Fairy Hill came into view, with the enchanted car park alongside.

"Don't the locals see the transport there and wonder?" asked the assistant assistant.

"Nah. All they see is a field full of sheep. Only those with the Sight, as a result of magical work, can see what's actually in the car park. They can all see the Hill, of course, but the entrance isn't easy to spot," replied Ned.

"So, the huge marble doors with all them columns around them aren't a bit of a give away then?" asked the junior, innocently.

"Only to us. Right. We need to try and spot either The Sleigh, or The Banned's mini bus. It's the same as last year, so you've both seen it before."

"Is that its licence plate?"

"What?"

"B 4?"

"Shut up."

Ned strode off into the Car Park.

"How are we going ter follow them, now that we've not got a car?" asked the assistant assistant, as he and the junior trailed behind Ned at a short distance.

"Dunno," replied the junior. "That's the Team Leader's problem. Tell you what though, I wouldn't have minded getting into the gig. The Banned always put a good set on."

And indeed, those Edern and assorted hangers on who were now spilling out of the Doorway past the disconsolate security frog were all in a good mood. Ned and his Team mixed with the crowd, and filtered their way slowly towards the back of the car park.

"Look!" hissed Ned, pointing. The Dark Wizards all hid behind a large, black estate car.

Eddie The Roadie loaded equipment into the minibus. The occasional crash floated across the air as a High Hat made a bid for freedom, objecting to receiving highhanded treatment from a non-musician. Eddie threw a couple of guitars in the back, slammed the doors and (with a grunt of effort) fastened the trailer back onto its hitch. The Banned trailed out to the bus, not looking too happy.

"I don't see why we don't just go home with the fee," grumbled

Scar.

"Do you want to explain that view to Grizelda?" asked Haemar.

"Leave me out of that one!" exclaimed GG hastily.

"Well, think of the benefits." Fungus cajoled his fellow Banned members.

"What benefits?" Felldyke mumbled through a chicken drumstick. A fast food group fast becoming his staple diet. That is, if he ate enough of them he would in time need staples to keep his clothes fastened together.

"Well, forget Grizelda for a moment."

"Wish I could." Haemar muttered, after quickly checking that she was not in hearing range. Or lip reading range. Or, indeed, frog range.

"We're actually helping our mates. Santa's Little Helpers. Who helped us. Who help Santa. So, come Christmas, you could look to get a little extra in the stocking, eh?"

"How little an extra?" asked GG suspiciously.

"Well, they're called Little Helpers, and they're all huge. So work it out."

Haemar started singing the chorus of *Mixed Emotions*, under his breath. The others were mentally weighing the situation, when Grizelda came round the corner of the Hill, followed by her goat and two reindeer, each blessed with huge antlers.

"I'm in," said Haemar quickly.

"Der," added Eddie, emphatically.

The Little Helpers trotted up anxiously.

"Well, guys? Can you help us?" pleaded Jerry, miserably.

The Banned found it hard to resist a miserable pleader, and so they all piled into the minibus. Mungo found it a bit hard to get in, until Bunsen bit the portion of Mungo that was sticking out of the door. Eddie slammed the door shut, and started the engine.

"Der?" he asked.

"South," answered Jerry.

Under Grizelda's approving gaze, the minibus and trailer left the car park.

"We need to follow them!" hissed Ned. He looked around, but the car park was emptying as the party-goers left.

"Right! We'll pinch this one." Ned looked around, then picked up a stone and broke the window of the large estate car behind which they were hiding. No one seemed to notice, so he opened the door and all three piled in, the assistant assistant driving.

"Any one know how to hot wire this?" asked Ned.

"Wouldn't matter if I did," answered the professional taxi driver. "The steering lock will be on too."

Ned swore, and then made a mystic pass with both hands over the steering column. There was a loud click, and the engine burst into life, and the steering lock disengaged.

"Where did you learn to do that?" asked the junior, impressed.

Ned sighed with exasperation. "We're supposed ter be Dark Wizards, yes? No damn good if we can't use our skills to steal cars when we need to, is it? Chapter Six in the manual, if you ever bother to read it. Now, follow that Sprinter, and don't stall it."

The dark estate eased through the traffic, out onto the main road after the Sprinter. The junior settled back in the back seat.

"What's on the CD?" he asked.

"It seems to be the soundtrack to The Rocky Horror Motion Picture Show."

"Great! I've not heard that in years. Is that the one with *Timewarp* in it?"

"Yeah," said the assistant assistant, looking at the CD cover, and nearly running over a passing sheep.

The junior looked behind him into the back of the car. "It's a big estate, this, Ned. There's four big wooden boxes in the back."

"Well, never mind them. Let's all concentrate on not losing that Sprinter."

"It's too dark for joggers, yet."

"Oh shut up. And turn up the music."

As the strains of *The Timewarp* filled the estate, the lid of one of the boxes quivered, shook, and unnoticed by the car thieves, started to open. A white hand emerged, and started fumbling around for the clasps.

Chapter Four

Grizelda watched the minibus carrying the Banned Underground leave the car park with a tinge of regret, for she was feeling a bit lonely. Normally she had a full and busy life, looking after a wayward husband, and a flatulent goat, and at the same time controlling her local coven and improving their flying abilities. The latter had improved to the point where the local airport had declared her training site an unofficial no-go zone after one aircraft had landed with an extremely irate witch caught on the tail fin by her cloak: it had been a good quality cloak, and the witch had been reluctant to let it go. The subsequent noisy disturbance on the airfield had been quelled by the arrival of Grizelda and a couple of the members of her coven. Harsh words had been exchanged, but those who had temporarily experienced the wonderful life of the frog no longer had a harsh word to say about Grizelda. Not in her hearing, anyway.

But all that had been left behind, to await her eager return, once she had finished her current special contract. With a sigh, she summoned the goat and picked up her broomstick from the pile of assorted weaponry that still littered the Doors of the Fairy Hill. The reindeer trotted up quietly behind her, with that special blend of cuteness and aggressive malice possessed only by those who come into frequent contact with small children.

Just as she kick started the broomstick – that is she dropped in on the floor, and kicked it until it started in sheer terror – a wail of despair came from the car park.

"Some beggar's stolen the Hearse!"

Grizelda sighed. The voice was familiar. Too familiar. She had been listening to it for the last four weeks, every other night, and the only thing that had stopped her from stopping the voice permanently was the enormous fee she was charging for listening to it complain.

"Now what?" she demanded, stamping across the car park to a small huddle of three cloaked and booted figures.

One spun round, hands raised and teeth bared, but very quickly backed down with apologies. And not just because of the glare from the reindeer, either. There was a certain amount of jostling, of the traditional kind.

"You tell her."

"You're the leader. It's your job."

"But I'm delegating it to you. That's leadership."

"Not setting a good example to us, are you?"

"She's tapping her foot. That's always a bad sign when she does taps her foot in my sessions."

"Oh, all right then."

The duly nominated one plastered what he hoped (without just cause) was a winning smile on his face.

"Ah, Grizelda. Good evening to you, and we all trust that you enjoyed the concert. Not the quite of thing that we ourselves would normally attend, of course, but jolly entertaining all the same."

"Wotcher, Count. What have yer done this time?" asked Grizelda.

"Well, we seem to have had an unfortunate occurrence," replied the Count.

"Where's yer car?"

"That is the question. Whilst we were doing our duty in the Fairy Hill, and supporting our friends and business contacts," started The Count.

"We were networking," clarified his aide, Percival.

"Making contacts," agreed Hugo, the third member of the trio.

"Making contact, too," smirked Percival, licking his lips. "But only consenting adults, of course," he added quickly, as Grizelda glared at him. He had no wish to be frogged. He already had enough problems being a vampire, and being a frog as well could be a little too much to bear.

"Get on with it," warned Grizelda, her foot still tapping. To *Foottapper* by the Shadows, a fill piece played by GG twenty minutes earlier.

"Well, we came out here to find the hearse gone."

"With our sleeping coffins still in it," explained Percival.

"And Dawn's coming," worried Hugo.

"She'll need a while longer yet." Grizelda reassured him, automatically, after a glance at the sky. She thought for a moment.

"Yer know, I think that I saw it driving out of the car park about 10 minutes ago. Could have been thieves, I suppose. Hey, where's your mate?"

Count Notveryfarout smiled, toothily. "He doesn't like bankers much. Not to his taste." The other vampires grinned alarmingly. "So he stayed in the hearse. I expect he will soon make himself known to whoever has been silly enough to steal it."

"But in the meantime..." muttered Hugo.

"But in the meantime, dawn is coming, so we need a place to

sleep."

"Well, I've got some spaces under the seats in the caravan." Grizelda sighed.

"We couldn't impose on you like that," smarmed The Count.

"Yes we can," said Percival, quickly.

Grizelda sighed, and picked up her broomstick. The owner of the caravan park had proved to be a little moody and parochial in his complaints about the goat. How he was going to cope with two reindeer, and three (at least well fed) vampires could well be a problem for her.

"Still," she mused to herself as she picked up the broomstick, "that is a problem for tomorrow." And there was a pond on site too. Whilst keen on her people/frog spell, Grizelda was also kind to amphibians on general principles. And so rarely kissed them.

As an afterthought, she turned and muttered something in the general direction of the security frog, who regained his proper shape. The guard looked around vaguely for his hat, and so missed the spectacle of a witch taking to the air (complete with tethered goat hanging below the broomstick), followed by an inflight formation of two reindeer and three vampires.

The late night regulars leaving the village pub a quarter of a mile away were however in a prime position to see and appreciate the formation take-off. It was a pity that they stood there; mouths agape, as the eldritch formation, reminiscent of the Red Arrows formation display team flew overhead flew overhead at 20 feet.* The reindeer yielded at once to the temptation.

* [The goat suffered from vertigo, and got airsick if Grizelda flew any higher whilst dangling the tethered goat under the broomstick.]

"That's disgusting," said Hugo in horror.

"They'll never get the stains out," agreed Percival.

"Stuff the stains. *The taste!*"

The flight was mercifully short; the landing took a little longer. Well, for Grizelda anyway, as the dew had made the grass a bit slippery.

"Well don't just stand there!" Grizelda demanded from underneath the caravan.

"Two of yer grab a boot each and pull me out!"

Averting their gaze, the vampires gulped, and then gingerly took hold of the boots (which were all that could be seen of Grizelda,) and pulled until the rest of her appeared, spoiling the view. Grumbling, Grizelda glared at the door of the caravan until it opened in sheer dread. With a courtly gesture, she waved the three vampires inside, and turned to the reindeer.

"Right you two, listen up. You can graze all around the caravan here. But no flying, no running off, and no terrorising the kiddies on the park. Oh, and watch out fer the owner. He's short, fat, bald and an idiot." Grizelda ordered.

The two reindeer looked at each other. She was spoiling their fun.

"Another day, and we'll find a way of keepin' you two busy and out of mischief," she assured them.

Bunsen and Burner looked at each other. They rather hoped that was impossible – given half a chance. Inside the caravan however, all was not well.

"You can't tell me she's living in this mess!" said Percival, horrified.

Hugo lifted up one of the beds, and peered into the black space below it. He sneezed, and vanished in a cloud of dust and goat hairs. "Oh good grief. She expects us to sleep in *here?*"

The Count examined his bed with distaste, but also a certain amount of resignation. Percival just stood still, the lid of the bed raised and an expression of horror and terror on his vampire face. What dread evil could he be facing, to frighten a vampire?

"It's her laundry. I can't sleep with her laundry! What if she wants to do washing during the day?"

Hugo joined him in examining the contents of the day bed.

"I shouldn't worry. I don't think any of this lot has been washed in ages. Look, those whites are definitely greys."

The Count came up with a solution. It wasn't soluble, but in his opinion it dissolved the difficulty.

"Hugo, get into your bed. We'll close the lid, then Percival can drop, can drop, can drop *those* onto the top of it, and get in his."

"What if they sort of filter down though?" asked Hugo. "I've already got all these goat hairs to contend with."

"We'll vacuum you off in the evening," reassured the Count, closing Hugo's lid on the complaints.

"You think Grizelda's going to have a vacuum cleaner?" came the muffled response.

Percival was searching his pockets anxiously.

"Now what have you lost?" demanded the Count, glancing out of the window. A faint gleam could now be seen on the horizon.

"Gloves. You think I'm going to pick up those with bare hands? I could be poisoned!"

"You're a vampire, for Gods' sakes. What can poison you?"

Percival looked pointedly at the pile of used underwear. The Count nodded. Maybe he had a point. Quickly The Count grabbed a cloth, and gathered the off-white pile into a heap, before dumping it on top of Hugo's day bed. Complaints arose from under the lid, but Percival jumped into his day bed and pulled the lid down after himself. The Count moved to his more select quarters, and also lay down to have a sleep

A few moments later Grizelda, having settled the goat and threatened the reindeer, also came into the caravan for a nap She examined the pile of laundry, which was overflowing the day bed onto the floor.

"I see they've tidied up a bit, at least," she muttered, before flinging herself down onto her bed at the rear of the caravan. Below her, The Count shuddered in fear and distaste, but then daylight overcame him and he knew no more.

Chapter Five

Dawn's early light shone gently on the summit of Allt y Cnicht, revealing a sombre group stood around The Sleigh. Haemar and GG were lying underneath the front part of The Sleigh, whilst Mungo anxiously waited to hear their verdict.

Felldyke wandered around to the back part of The Sleigh, but as he leant against it part of the woodwork snapped. The loud crack made everyone turn and stare at him, and he grinned sheepishly. The sheep grinned back at him, but he ignored them.

"Well, what do you think?" Mungo asked.

Haemar slid slowly out from underneath, whilst GG still prodded about with his screwdriver, examining the electrics. "Technically, or in layman's terms?" he replied.

Mungo and Jerry looked at each other, then back at Haemar. Jerry shrugged.

Haemar copied him. "Either way, it's the same answer. It's knackered. The ellipsoid mounting plate for the multi drive connect and feedback delivery system has sheared away and taken with it the epicyclic torque condenser and waste energy recovery unit, otherwise known as the afterburner. Oh, and the right hand ski runner is under three feet of peat bog."

There then came a loud fizzing noise, abruptly cut off, and a small cloud of smoke appeared from under the front of The Sleigh, rapidly followed by GG, his eyebrows on fire, and carrying a small blowtorch in one hand.

"I found the afterburner!" he announced, waving the blowtorch (which was in fact the afterburner). "It's supposed ter be fitted to the front of The Sleigh, but it had come off. That's probably why you lost power."

"Can you fix it?" asked Jerry.

Haemar shook his head slowly. "Sorry, mate. Maybe if we had the right tools we could do something. But with this, it's not just about bolting the bits back on."

GG nodded glumly. "The electrics are a bit shot, but I could do something there for you. Problem is, though, this is The Sleigh."

"So?" asked Mungo.

"Well," GG carried on, "there's a lot of complicated circuitry to do with its special needs."

"It has ter go extra fast, and be invisible," Haemar explained. "That's not all about mechanics, there's some spell work too. That's why you need yer specialist, who's got the manual."

"I thought that it was all automatic?" asked Boris, confused by the technicalities.

Haemar looked at him blankly.

"The workshop manual," explained GG to Boris.

"So" said Fungus brightly, "all we need to do is get it down of this hilltop, and over to the mechanic. Who is he?"

"Erm. You know that guy we took you to see last year when your van broke down?" muttered Jerry.

The Banned froze. "Not the Vampire Mechanic?" asked Scar,

slowly.

"Yes, him. Idiot. Basil."

"Basil? What sort of name is that for a vampire?" asked GG, confused.

"'Sright," agreed Scar. "They normally all have posh names, like Count something."

"Count what?" asked Felldyke.

"Count anything," replied GG, in agreement with Scar for once.

"Well, there's only one Sleigh, there's four of these guys,"

"Shut up Felldyke."

The drummer subsided, confused.

"He's trying to appear normal," explained Mungo, referring to Basil.

"Nobody called Basil is normal," complained Scar. "Look at that hotel in Torquay we stayed in last year. The manager was called Basil."

The Banned all nodded in agreement. The Hotel manager had indeed been on the borderline of clinical insanity, with a regular visitor visa in his passport.

"Is the mechanic still in that same place?" asked Fungus.

"I've forgotten where that was," said Scar with relief.

"Der," agreed Eddie.

"Don't worry, we know where to go," reassured Mungo.

"Der."

"There's no need for that language," replied Jerry.

"He's probably a bit upset," said Fungus.

"And not the only one," grumbled Haemar. "Grizelda could have told us."

"What, and spoil the surprise?" asked Boris. "Listen, we helped you out last year, all you need to do is help us now, and you've repaid the favour."

The Banned glared at him. They knew that there was an implied threat (other than Grizelda) going on, they just couldn't see it yet.

Mungo sighed. "Look lads, falling out will get us nowhere."

"We're already there," grumbled Haemar looking around at the desolate hilltop.

"Let's think logically," suggested Fred. There was a stunned silence, and everyone turned to look at him.

"Well, it's pretty obvious to me," Fred continued. "The Sleigh isn't going to work until we can get it to Idiot. Basil. At the bottom of the hill we've got, thanks to our mates here," (The Banned all looked around until they realised he meant them) "a van and a trailer. So, all we need to do is get the Sleigh to the trailer, and then drive to Idiot's place."

Jerry looked at Fred with his mouth open. "I've known you for what, three hundred years, and that's probably the first time you've ever said anything sensible."

GG wandered over to the edge of the hill. "It's about five hundred feet down to the van," he said.

"Easy then," said Fungus. "We shove it over the edge, and run after it until it stops."

"Will it fly downwards under control?" asked Scar.

"We'll put Jerry in it to see," suggested Boris, an idea that met a lot of popular support.

"Look," Jerry said quickly, "the Sleigh isn't going to work, so it won't go properly."

"It's only got ter fly down though," Haemar agreed. "Even stones do that."

Felldyke and Scar went to the back of the Sleigh, and started pushing. In a moment or so, with a very unpleasant noise (that caused Fungus to have a fit of nostalgia, as a BogTroll) it started to slide forwards towards the edge of the hill. With a certain level of peer pressure, and a poke from the sharp sword Haemar just happened to find in his hand, Jerry was persuaded aboard. GG and the rest of Santa's Little Helpers joined Felldyke and Scar, pushing at the rear.

"Hang on, whilst I try to fire up the systems!" yelled Jerry, but too late: with a last heave the Sleigh slid over the edge of the hill, and quickly accelerated downwards. Jerry urgently started pressing buttons on the control console. For a moment, he was so busy he forgot to yell abuse back over his shoulder, until he realised that doing so gave him an opportunity not to look where he was going...

A golden haze surrounded the Sleigh, which promptly backfired twice, setting the heather on the hillside on fire. Mungo and Boris ran down the slope, and found an organic way to put out the small fires, whilst Fred sat on a rock and laughed. Cautiously, The Banned walked down the hill in the wake of the Sleigh, now nearly at the bottom of the slope.

"Der! Der!" remarked Eddie.

GG patted his arm. "Don't worry, I think that it's going to miss yer van."

"Der! Der!"

"Ah. Well, maybe not then."

"Der!"

But Eddie sighed in relief as the Sleigh shot towards the Sprinter, then when a collision seemed unavoidable, bounced off a large rock, sailed over the top of the Sprinter, and with golden sparks flying in all directions made a heavy landing on the far side.

"Do you think Jerry will be OK?" panted Scar, as the whole party ran anxiously downwards.

The volume and inventiveness of the cursing rising up the slope was, on the whole, reassuring, until it stopped. The Banned and the remaining Little Helpers reached the Sprinter, and paused for breath. The Sleigh lay on the other side of the minibus, having suffered little or no noticeable additional damage from the trip down the hill. It was empty.

"Jerry! Jerry! Are you OK?" yelled Fred, panting from the efforts of the run down the hill.

"Where do yer reckon he is, then?" wondered Scar, looking underneath the Sprinter.

"Well, he must have been here," said Felldyke, "what with all the yelling."

"Mmmmmmmmmm" observed Jerry, unseen.

"That's him!" sighed Mungo, in some relief.

"Mmmmmm!!!"

"Perhaps he's lost the power of speech?" suggested Boris.

"We don't get that lucky," replied Fred. "Oh look, there he is." He pointed at a dark shape, which on closer inspection turned out to be their comrade, partly buried in a peat bog, with an enormous lump of grass clogging his mouth.

"MMMmmmmMMM!" Jerry suggested.

"He seems a bit fed up to me," said Fungus.

"Don't see why," grumbled Felldyke. "He had a ride down the hill, we had ter do it on foot."

"Should we pull that mud out of his mouth? What if he chokes?" asked Scar.

The other Little Helpers looked at each other. "Leave him that way for a bit," suggested Boris. Fred nodded.

"Can't complain so much like that, can he?"

"*MMMMmmmmmmmmmM!!*"

"Maybe he can, after all."

"Come on," called Haemar. He and Eddie had moved the van and trailer up beside the Sleigh whilst the others had clustered around Jerry. With a chorus of grumbles and complaints they all heaved, pulled, lifted and hauled until the Sleigh sat on top of the trailer, and Eddie started securing it with ropes.

"Right!" said Fred. "All we need to do now it drive to the workshop, and we're on the way, lads."

They all squashed into the Sprinter, and Eddie drove off into the night, or what was left of it.

"What's on the CD?" asked Fungus, settling back in the front with Haemar.

"*Highway Star.*"

"That'll do nicely."

"Mmmmmmm"

"Someone pull the mud out of his mouth, now."

The mud was removed, but quickly reinstated when the cursing started again.

"Doesn't know when ter shut up, your mate, does he?" grumbled Felldyke.

"No," replied Boris. "His mouth is always getting us into trouble back home, too."

"I've always wondered," asked Felldyke cautiously, "what's it like living at Santa's place?"

"Well, I suppose it's not bad. We have a lot better time these days, as more of the functions are automated, and now when there's a proper cock-up, we can always blame the computer. It gets pretty dull though, because a lot of the time there's not much to do but monitor the toy acquisition systems, maintain the delivery lists, and muck out the reindeer."

"Do what with the reindeer?"

"Well, it's basically a horse, with an even worse attitude and a dodgy digestion. And damn big sharp horns. So, we have a huge muck heap."

"How do yer get rid of it?"

"Well, Notsanta's round helps. We use quite a bit of it there. And Himself is into organic gardening, so we compost a lot. But occasionally we have to fire it." Boris paused to choke with laughter. "We did that one year, and it went up so fast that the flames affected the ozone layer."

Felldyke frowned. "Weren't that a bit antisocial?"

"No, it kept a couple of thousand Climatologists in jobs for ten years or so, and saved a fortune."

"How did it do that?"

"They thought all their Christmases had come at once, so we took them off the delivery Round for ages."

Felldyke nodded, and chose to doze whilst Eddie drove the Sprinter into the dawn.

"I'm not driving us up that lane!" insisted the assistant assistant.

Ned examined the entrance to the unsurfaced and unmarked lane, and had to agree. "I think yer right. We'd never turn this huge thing round in a hurry if we had to."

"It is a bit big," agreed the junior. He looked around in the gloomy rear of the hearse, but saw nothing except the four silent boxes. "Got ter say though, these boxes give me the creeps."

"Why?" asked the assistant assistant whilst Ned frantically examined the map to see where the lane led to.

"I keep feeling something might creep out of them."

"They're just boxes. What's going ter creep out of them then?"

"Besides me, you mean?" asked a smooth voice.

There was a certain level of stillness inside the vehicle.

"Here, Bill," said the assistant assistant, a little nervously, "I didn't know you could speak posh like that."

"I thought it were Ned? Boss, tell me it was you!"

"Er, no," Ned said very slowly, letting the map fall to the floor.

"Of course it wasn't. That's because it was me," said the voice from the rear of the hearse.

"I was frightened someone were going to say that," the assistant assistant said slowly.

"Be aware," Ned tried to be authoritative despite the efforts of his intestines, "we are Dark Wizards and have many strange powers. Fear to mess us about!"

The junior felt a pressure on the back seat, and very slowly turned to his right. "If I open my eyes, what am I going to see?" he quavered.

"Life can be such an adventure, can't it?" the voice replied, smoothly. "Not as I'd know now," it added, a trace of bitterness creeping into the tone. For some reason, the junior failed to feel reassured by this. Nor by the cold hand reassuringly patting his arm.

Ned flexed his hexing fingers, and turned to look into the dim recess of the rear. "Who exactly are you, then?" he demanded of the well-dressed figure sat uncomfortably close to the junior.

"My name's Basil. I'm a mechanic. And the owner of this vehicle. Oh, I nearly forgot to mention it, but I'm a Vampire as well."

There came a silence, as all three wizards thought carefully about their next sentence.

"Excuse me, Sir," the assistant assistant managed to croak. "It isn't long until dawn. Would you not be safer, er, somewhere dark?"

"You are course correct," Basil replied. "My thoughts almost entirely. I just have to decide whether I'm going to kill you all first or not."

"Ah," said Ned. "Is there anything we might say to help influence your decision? We are after all both Dark Wizards and accountants."

"I've never seen the difference myself," agreed Basil. "But as it happens, I could use some help in that regard. I've had this letter from the tax office, you see."

Ned nodded wisely.

"So, I am prepared to propose a compromise for now."

"Yes?" asked the junior, noticing how Basil's hand no longer lay reassuringly on his arm, but now reassured his shoulder (close to his neck, as it happened) instead.

"You see, if I were to kill you now, which would be the easiest option..."

"Maybe for you," grumbled the assistant assistant. Basil acknowledged the point with a toothy grin.

"Then I would not be able to drive home before dawn. And this vehicle is not one I would like to leave stranded in a car park.

Someone might steal it."

"Surely not? Who would be that stupid?" croaked the junior.

"Well, you lot were. Or, you could drive me to a prearranged spot, where you could either leave me or wait until tomorrow night, when we could converse more."

"That's favourite for me," agreed Ned.

"Done," smiled Basil. "Here is my business card. Please drive the hearse there."

"You'd trust us?" the assistant assistant asked.

"Oh yes. You see, these other three coffins are empty."

"Why would we be scared of an empty coffin?" asked Ned.

Basil smiled, and again his long fangs were somehow quite noticeable. "Because their owners will hunt you down and then become rather imaginative, should I be – let us say, harmed. Plus, my main employer will take a lengthy and extremely evil revenge upon your persons."

"Who is your employer, then?"

"I contract for Santa."

The three wizards looked at each other.

"Funny, there seem to be lots of people working for Santa," mused Ned.

"Dyslexia was very common a few hundred years ago."

"You said you are a mechanic, sir?" ventured the junior.

"Indeed."

"Then, sir," smiled Ned, "You are the object of our Quest, and be assured that we will not seek to harm you in any way. Our Boss has sent us on a mission, and we need to talk to you at length."

The Vampire Mechanic patted his pockets with both hands, causing the junior to faint in relief at the removal of Basil's hand from his neck, and fall across the vampire's lap.

"I hate it when they do that," complained Basil in annoyance, and not too gently shoved the junior onto the floor. "Panders to socio stereotyping. Here." He thrust a small printed sheet at Ned, who took it carefully. "My rates. See you in the morning."

The Vampire Mechanic climbed back into his box, and closed the lid. Ned and the assistant assistant could clearly hear the sound of heavy clasps snapping shut on the outside, followed by more clasps on the inside.

Ned ran his eyes down the printed sheet. "Let's see. Clutches £ 200 plus parts. Basic Service £ 150 plus parts. Major service £400 plus parts. Metaphysical discussions, £ 200 per hour. All prices plus tax."

"No wonder he's a vampire. Those prices are bloodsucking," commented the erstwhile taxi driver.

"Right. Now, we've got all day to make some plans, let's find somewhere to lurk."

"Look, Ned! The Banned are coming along the track towards us!"

And indeed in the half-light, the distant shape of the Sprinter could be seen approaching.

"Right!" said Ned.

"The track is on the left, Ned."

"No, you idiot, just drive out of their way, and turn round as fast as you can. Then follow them at a discreet distance."

"Discreet? With this? I'll have ter be so far behind them that we'll be on different pages of your map."

But Ned was looking at the printed sheet he was holding and smiling. "No worries. I think that I know where they're going better than they do."

"Ah. You mean, they're using a SatNav and we're just following them?"

"No. This time, we're not going to get lost at all."

The SatNav maintained an uninjured silence. That is, it stayed silent and so stayed uninjured, too.

Chapter Six

The caravan vibrated. It shook. It rattled, and occasionally rolled back and forth. No mean feat for a wheeled trailer thirty-six feet long, normally moved by a tractor. The energy needed could have powered the whole campsite for half a day, and came from a renewable, and possibly green resource: Grizelda was snoring. Outside, even the reindeer had retreated, and a small crowd made up from the other residents on the site had collected. They were all looking at the site owner, a small, bald, stooped and pot-bellied figure, who was twisting his hands together like a modern Mr Micawber.

A mighty effort made several of the windows in the nearby caravan shake and a nearby dustbin fell over, much to the delight and interest of the reindeer.

"You've got to do something," one visitor told the site owner (known as Dai The Park) who looked worried. As well he might.

"We're not safe in our beds," complained a middle-aged leviathan from London who would have been safe in anything up to a small nuclear explosion.

"Got to think of the kiddies on the park," agreed another.

The Reindeer looked up. They were always interested in children, although normally as a possible addition to their diet.

"Right, right," agreed Dai The Park, looking determined and long suffering in turns, and finally settling for shifty.

"Look, what's the worst she can do?" asked the first visitor, fiercely. "Shout at you a bit? Poke you with a brush? She's just a middle aged old bag, not a witch or something!"

"Er," replied Dai The Park, who was not overly convinced by this line of reasoning. The caravan shook again on its chassis.

"If you won't, I will!" exclaimed a brawny builder from Birmingham He was afraid of almost nothing except mice, but they had fled the vicinity complaining of severe headaches from the noise pollution, leaving him (in his opinion) unchallengeable. He stepped boldly up to the door, and silence, a blessed silence, fell. The lady leviathan looked disappointed, and Dai The Park was relieved. The builder turned away, and as he did so another gargantuan snore was released, and Dai The Park found himself relieved again, although in a rather different fashion. The builder jumped, and some fabric gave way under the stress.

"That's torn it!" howled the brawny builder, and hammered on the door of Grizelda's van with the hand not employed in keeping his torn modesty intact.

"See?" he demanded from his audience, and then turned back to the door. He raised a mighty fist, but froze as his glare was met by Grizelda's higher wattage version at a range of five centimeters.

"Yes?" she enquired sweetly, as the brawny builder toppled slowly backwards, landing in something soft and brown, carefully deposited earlier by the reindeer.

"Er," remarked the builder.

"Um, Miss Dorothy," stammered Dai The Park. The laser-like glare turned slowly to aim between his eyes, and he swallowed hard. "We, er, we, we were worried about you. There was this noise, you see."

"Noise? What sort of noise?"

"You were snoring!" insisted the leviathan, striding like a modern Genghis Khan across the field towards Grizelda.

"Me? Snoring? I never were!"

"You were snoring so loudly that your whole caravan was shaking. And these horses of yours were scared."

Grizelda instantly assumed that the whole statement was a lie, on the very reasonable grounds that she could think of nothing in North Wales, not even the inhabitants, that was capable of scaring those Reindeer.

"I don't believe it. I were only having a nap. If I'd been snoring, I'd have heard it meself."

"Um, miss?" asked Dai The Park, his hands twisting together fast enough to generate as much heat as a small incinerator, "You can't hear yourself snore, because you'd be asleep, and, well, you wouldn't be listening."

Grizelda snorted like a reindeer. "Rubbish, man, rubbish. Now let me finish my nap in peace!"

She turned, and retreated inside. The builder squirmed on the floor, realised what he was lying in, and swore inventively. Dai The Park stopped twisting his hands together, and put them in his pockets, which promptly burst into flames from the heat.

"Ow!" he shouted, and jumped about beating at the flames with his hands, before jumping into the nearby pool.

The leviathan hammered her fist on Grizelda's door, with a thunderous expression. Two seconds later she rocked forwards as the door was flung open, then rocked backwards as a hooked nose and a steely gaze locked with her more bucolic expression, and then she turned green. And hopped into the pool.

"Rivet, rivet" she exclaimed mournfully. Dai The Park vanished under the water, and the burly builder crab-walked backwards away from the glare.

"Dai!" demanded Grizelda.

A stream of bubbles from under the surface of the water betrayed the site owner's presence.

"Do you sell them 'Do Not Disturb' signs in yer overpriced shop, then?"

The bubbles seemed to have a metaphysically negative quality about them. Grizelda glared all around at the rapidly clearing space before her door.

"I dunno. What a girl has ter do to get a bit of piece and quiet." The door slammed shut behind her. Dai The Park cautiously arose from the murky depths of the pool, and discovered a small green frog was perched on his head. With a pop, the frog returned to being the London leviathan, and at once both she and Dai vanished under the water again, to emerge dripping wet and furious with each other.

A few minutes later, the field before the caravan door was again deserted, and vibrating gently. But Grizelda, as is so often the case, found it impossible to sleep properly now that she had been so thoroughly awakened. She climbed back out of the bed, grumbling at the amount of daylight that found its reluctant way through the inadequate curtains, and changed into some nearly fresh clothes. The removed garments joined the small mountain of items waiting to go to the laundry.

The refrigerator in the caravan was a safer item than the version she had at home, and opened to the gentle persuasion of a heavy boot with few complaints and certainly no backchat or threats. The milk however had been there for some time, and was now in a belligerent mood, and snapped at her hand as it snaked past into the depths, before emerging with the butter.

"Full English, that's what I need," she muttered to herself, and glared at the stove until the gas ignited. She slammed the frying pan onto the flames, and went back into the fridge for the sausages. "Hum, green bits. Probably herbs, I should think." She started to put the sausages into the rapidly heating oil, then remembered and stopped at three.

"I know that he had ter stay for his job, but I do miss him," she muttered to herself. Ben, her long suffering husband served as the outlet for her frustrations (she could shout at him as much as she wanted, ever since he had developed selective deafness in self defense, and since he was a wizard he was able to deflect the hexes she fired at him, unless he happened to be drunk – when they usually failed to take effect anyway.

"Still, only a couple more weeks ter go, and my time with this Count and his crew is up. He'll have to offer me a shed load of money to stay on, I think that I've had enough of them and their stupid problems. Depressed vampires. Whoever heard the like? And it's not as if it isn't because of poor diet and all. All that B Negative blood they get round here. Time they moved on."

The hot oil sizzled around the sausages, which moved slightly in the pan as the virulent bacteria gave up the fight to survive. Grizelda turned them, then cracked open an egg or two and sent them into the pan to join the sausages. A piece of bread followed, and began turning slowly black.

"Not as much fun, cooking for one," muttered Grizelda. "Dunno how that Delia Smith had the nerve to write about it. And I don't suppose this lot of dozy vampires would want any, either."

The* aroma drifted around the interior of the caravan. Even in his death-like daytime state, the Count twitched in horror and distaste.

*[for want of a more accurate word that would leave the author unfrogged]

"Brown sauce.* Can't be doing with that ketchup stuff, spoils the taste." Grizelda picked up a plate, and wiped it on her sleeve. The resulting combination of bacteria subsequently bred a new virus capable of wiping out all life on earth, until the witch blew her nose on her sleeve, and eradicated all traces of it forever.

*[Other sauces are available. This aside is in the spirit of inclusivity and celebration of diversity now informing all areas of life and is to protect the publisher and author from being sued by the lawyers for rival condiment manufacturers.]

The Full English Breakfast (which is normally restricted to tea, toast, marmalade and domestic disharmony, but Grizelda considered her present circumstances deserving of a little more) slid out of the frying pan and onto the plate next to the small lake of brown sauce, and Grizelda raised her knife and fork.

Outside the caravan, a slowly spreading puddle of water evidenced the presence of the site owner, who was carefully peering through a window to see if it was safe to knock on the door again. His full concentration was employed in this exceptionally (for him) courageous deed, and so he failed to hear the stealthy steps of the untethered Reindeer.

"Mebbe I'll put some music on," decided Grizelda. Munching happily, she reached across and turned on the radio. The inane burbling of the presenter faded away, to be replaced by the unmistakeable tones of Haemar's opening howl, as the DJ played the Banned's version of 'Jumping Jack Flash', successfully obscuring the howl from Dai The Park as the Reindeer propelled him over the top of the caravan to a soft landing in the smelly spot earlier vacated by the builder. Grumbling, Dai staggered away.

When she had nearly washed up her breakfast things, Grizelda contemplated her day. This would be the first for some time in daylight, as she was normally awake for much of the night earning her fees by trying to cure the vampires of their depression. A noise outside disturbed her train of thought, and she looked out of the window. Across the park, in the next field, some girls from the local Pony Club were riding their horses, watched by proud and anxious parents. The Reindeer, she thought. She could exercise the reindeer, and that might give her a few sorely needed brownie points with her coven leader. Grizelda was well aware that her reputation, like her smalls, was far from spotless and she really did want to get a place on the summer conference this year. Which could be unlikely unless she improved her performance rating.

"Those Dark Wizards at Caer Surdin get it so much easier," she mused, and felt a flicker of temptation to join the Dark Side, and their cookies. But then dismissed it. Being good wasn't easy, she felt, but still the right thing for her. Maybe. Determined, she pulled on her heaviest boots, and stomped out of the van to investigate. "You know, it's been a long time since you rode anything but that broomstick," she said aloud, but to herself. "One of them would be different, and something ter boast about back at the Coven. None of *them*, not even that stuck-up cow Maddy, will have ridden on one of Himself's Reindeer. OK, then, let's go see."

Across the park, in the next field, the Pony Club show jumping competition was proceeding in the traditional fashion for such local community events. One mother had threatened to punch another competitor's mother, both had determined to give the Judge a piece of their minds, and neither of them were speaking to the mother whose daughter was presently winning the competition. One of the assorted fathers was busy letting down the tyres on a horsebox belonging to his local business rival, who in turn was taking the opportunity to steal some of the first father's customers by slandering his business practices to them. Several of the other fathers had abandoned watching the children altogether to sit around the onsite catering and argue passionately about the mindless violence in football, thereby avoiding the mindless violence that was ready to erupt around the show ring. Grizelda stood at the side of the field and nodded happily. She was going to fit right in.

"Ladies and gentlemen," said the announcer into his far too quiet PA system, "The judges are going to take their lunch break, then we will move on to the adult classes, starting with the novice jumping."

Grizelda turned, and hurried off towards the reindeer. Now, should she ride Bunsen, or Burner? She found the two reindeer close to the caravan site toilets. They had chased three small children inside, and were having fun keeping them prisoners. One of the closed doors now bore a firm hoof print, which was probably a sign of good luck.

"Come away, you two!" she ordered, and the Reindeer, with a backward glance or two, followed her back to the caravan.

"Right. You need to have some exercise whilst them idiots what brought you here get The Sleigh sorted out."

The Reindeer looked at her, then at each other doubtfully, then back at Grizelda.

"So, I'm going ter ride you."

This time the look of derision on the Reindeers' faces was unmistakeable. Grizelda cracked her finger joints, "Now, I've never changed one of you lot into a frog, but there's a first time fer everything. Do we ride, or do yer spend the afternoon hopping about in the pond?"

The Reindeer gave each other a long look, and then trotted reluctantly behind the stumpy figure of the witch.

"Right," she said. "Now, we all know you don't need these reins, but we are going to have ter fit them for the look of the thing." The Reindeer nodded morosely. They didn't think that the witch's spell would work on them, but were unwilling to road test the hypothesis. Grizelda picked up the bridle she had filched from an empty horsebox, and Burner shied in alarm. Bunsen bared his teeth, but found to his dismay that he had made it easier for Grizelda to fit the hateful thing in his mouth and over his head.

"Good!" said Grizelda, in blatant defiance of the evidence. She threw a cloth over Bunsen's back, and leapt aboard. "You, wait here!" she instructed Burner, and pointed at the Pony Club field. Bunsen nodded glumly, and trotted off. A wide, but closed, gate stood at the corner where the two fields met: and a very bored parent was slumped in a chair beside the hedge with a flask of coffee at his side, officially Warden of The Gate. Grizelda's attempt at a demure cough roused him gently from his doze. Bunsen poking him in the short ribs with his antlers had a more urgent effect.

"What? What? What is *that?*"

"Here's a clue. It has four legs, a bridle, and I'm riding it."

"That's NOT a horse."

Grizelda leant forward and smiled. "Do you want to tell him?"

Bunsen pawed the ground, and shook his antlers. The warden

opened the gate as quickly as he could, to let them in.

The announcer cleared his throat, a lengthy process after the picnic his wife had made for his lunch. "Class Forty-one, I say Class Forty-one!" he croaked into the microphone for the PA system. "Working Hunter Jumping, for Native Ponies."

Grizelda looked up, interested. Bunsen was a working animal and definitely a native of somewhere. This could be the competition she was looking for, and it would certainly be fun. She shook the reins slightly, and Bunsen trotted up towards the bit of the field set out for the Working Hunter course. All around was a throng of horses of various sizes and shapes, carrying more or less interchangeable children and attached by lead ropes to decidedly interchangeable and complaining mothers. Bunsen moved through the milling crowd easily, occasionally clearing his way by prodding a pony or attached mother with his horns. The unlikely partnership arrived at the start line, and was inspected by an open-mouthed lady holding a piece of rope.

"Is this the start?" asked Grizelda, politely.

"Er... what sort of horse is this?" asked the steward.

"Who are you?"

"I'm the steward for this ring."

"Good!" exclaimed Grizelda, "I'll need a drink afterwards."

"No, I'm the steward for the judge, her assistant really, and I sort out the entries. What sort of horse is this, then?"

"Fancy you not knowing that. It's, it's, it's a Laplander."

"That's not on my list here. I'll have to ask the judge."

"Fine, we'll do that together then, shall we?" agreed Grizelda.

The open-mouthed lady looked like she was about to object, but Bunsen lowered his antlers in a suggestive fashion, and she decided to pass the buck, as it were. The unlikely ensemble walked slowly into the ring, Grizelda looking around as memories from her childhood surged through her mind. Prominent amongst these was the pompous judge she had once met at a Pony Club event. The lady judging this competition was uncannily alike Grizelda's memory, even down to the pink creation with tall heels she had chosen to wear into what was basically a farmer's field, with extra mud added.

"What is this?" the judge enquired, in tones so aristocratic that the steward curtsied from her inbuilt racial memories.

"He's called Bunsen," Grizelda said amicably. "He's a Laplander."

"There's no such breed," declaimed the judge, in a haughty fashion, as if that ended the discussion, and turned her immaculate back on them. The steward shrugged, apologetically.

"Sorry, there you are, no entry, I'm afraid."

Bunsen had now decided that some jumping might actually be fun, so he moved sideways a little. By sheer chance, one very heavy hoof landed on the steward's foot. Her scream was loud enough to make the judge turn around, annoyed at the intrusion into her authority. She glared fiercely at Grizelda, who returned the stare.

"Please leave the ring," the judge insisted. Grizelda turned up the wattage on her glare, to be amazed when it had no effect.

"I have asked you to leave," remarked the judge dismissively, and turned her back towards Grizelda again. Bunsen gently removed her enormous hat, and with every sign of enjoyment, began eating it.

"That's my hat! My hat! Make your animal give it back!" demanded the judge, whilst the steward tried to hide behind her clipboard. At the side of the ring, a small crowd had gathered – one mother gave Bunsen a muted cheer, but was quickly smothered by the other parents, who were terrified of reprisals. Bunsen looked at Grizelda, who nodded. Bunsen hiccupped twice, and then sicked the munched pieces of hat up onto the elegant and expensive shoes worn by the judge. Grizelda meekly handed the uneaten remains of the hat back. Bunsen grabbed the steward's clipboard, and started eating that instead.

"I have made my decision, and that's that," insisted the judge, cramming the drooping and drool coated remains of her hat onto her head.

Grizelda leant forward. "Is there some room ter negotiate?"

"No. Go Away. Rivet, rivet, rivet."

The steward stared at the new, pink coloured frog in horror. "You can't do that to a judge!" she exclaimed.

"Why not?" asked Grizelda.

"Well, because, because, what if everyone started doing it?"

"Maybe they'd be a bit less pompous."

"Don't be silly. They are judges. They go on this special training course. One day on how to judge the horses, one day on being pompous and pretentious in all circumstances, one day in never ever admitting that you are wrong. About anything. And not lifting a finger in a ring until you are sure that you are getting a decent lunch given you for free."

"Rivet, rivet!" remarked the frog, rejecting some flies as lacking enough style to be eaten.

Grizelda, who never admitted to being wrong either, saw the problem straight away. "You mean she might not let me go round even if I stop her being a frog."

"It's possible. She's a judge. It's hard enough getting them to make a decision in the first place, let along change it. We had one competitor hurt here last year."

"What, they had an accident?"

"Sort of. She fell off her horse after she fell asleep waiting for a judge's decision."

"Landed on her head, I presume."

"She'd have been fine if she did that. No, she landed on the judge, and got kicked quite badly."

"Ah. Well, let's see if she has changed her mind yet."

Grizelda nodded at the frog and the judge reappeared, a little green around the edges, in a tasteful contrast to her pink outfit. The judge drew herself up to her full five feet two inches of height, but the effect was rather spoiled when her high heels sank into the soft ground and she tilted backwards alarmingly before coming to rest at a twenty-degree angle.

"Never touched her!" protested Grizelda.

The judge tried to clear her head of an urgent desire to catch flies, and agreed that Grizelda could compete, to a lot of muttered complaints from outside the ring.

"Are you going to walk the course?" the steward asked.

"No, I'm going ter ride round it. That's why I've got Bunsen," replied Grizelda, confused.

"No, I mean do you want to walk around the course before you ride round it?"

"Do yer get extra points for it?"

"Er, no. But most riders find it helps to know the order to jump the jumps," suggested the steward.

"I don't give Bunsen orders. He's pretty good at finding his way around on his own."

"Er, right. Well, the jumps are numbered anyway, so good luck."

The judge nodded vaguely, still focussing on the collection of flies hanging round the remains of her hat. Grizelda whispered in Bunsen's ear, and the Reindeer accelerated to his easy canter, and started round the course. Possibly an experienced rally driver could have matched his speed, but his car might have struggled with the jumps. Bunsen did not.

"How were that then?" asked Grizelda, as Bunsen trotted up to the judge and halted, showering the steward in mud.

"I don't think that I've ever seen anything like it before," stammered the judge. She held out her hand, and the steward put some rosettes into it.

"I'm going to have to give you first prize, and say that you have qualified to go to the big championships in a few weeks' time." Grizelda smirked, and Bunsen looked very self satisfied.

The judge, still disorientated from her recent experience as a frog, held out the qualification card and first place rosette. Bunsen made a lunge for them, but Grizelda was faster. She grabbed both, nodded to the judge and steward, and made Bunsen trot out of the ring. On the way, she fed him the rosette, to appalled comments from the audience of riders and mothers, many of whom would have happily killed and eaten someone else's daughter for the winner's rosette. And waded through a river of blood (although in a ladylike fashion) for the qualification card in Grizelda's pocket...

Ignoring the scandalised mutterings, and the fist fight in the car park (the deflated tyres on the horsebox had been discovered), Grizelda trotted Bunsen happily back to the caravan site, her good temper quite restored.

Chapter Seven

The hearse drove into the soft morning light, some distance behind the glowing taillights of the trailer attached to the Sprinter minibus. As the sun, panting a little from the exertion, rose above the stark mountains of Snowdonia, the junior wizard finally relaxed.

"Ned," he said, "tell me again why we still have a vampire in the back?"

"Well, we're supposed ter be on the side of utmost evil, aren't we?"

"I thought we were part time accountants," replied Bill.

"And I'm supposed ter be a taxi driver," said Ben.

"See?" explained Ned. "Proof positive!"

"What?"

"When did you last meet an angelic taxi driver?"

"Suppose you have a point," muttered the junior wizard. The assistant assistant looked outraged. "But, why have we got a Vampire? Listen, he doesn't care if we are goodies or baddies, does he?"

Ned sighed, theatrically. "Look, you muppet, that's not just *any* common or garden vampire."

"No vampires in my garden," retorted the assistant assistant. "Me wife would have a lot ter say about it if we had."

"Your wife has a lot ter say about everything," muttered the junior.

"Tell me about it. I can't wait until I'm allowed Spellbook 2."

"Why?" asked the junior, who had only just been allowed it himself.

"There's meant ter be this spell in it that stills nagging tongues."

Ned shook his head. "Tongues of NAGS. It's to keep horses quiet, not yer missus."

The assistant assistant was unfazed. "She's got a face like a horse, so with any luck it will still work."

"I never understood why you married her," ventured the junior.

"Actually, she talked me into it."

"Seems likely," agreed Ned. "Twenty minutes of listening to her, you'd agree ter anything for a bit of quiet."

"Is that why yer joined up with Caer Surdin, then?" asked the junior.

The assistant assistant nodded. "Being an evil wizard is better even than having a shed at bottom of the garden. She could just open kitchen window and yell at me there. Doing this is like going on holiday."

The junior was confused. "But we don't know quite where we are going, we've no luggage and a limited spending budget for food (although the beer kitty is OK) and we aren't sure how we are getting home again."

"See?" said the assistant assistant. "Just like a package holiday, isn't it? When's the next pub stop?"

"We are following our duty to our Coven Leader, not on a pub crawl!" objected Ned.

Both the junior and the assistant assistant smiled. They knew that following The Banned would mean a pub break before too long. Ned reached into his pocket, and fished out the SatNav. Connecting the power cable, he pushed the power switch.

After a few moments, words blurred across the screen, which stabilised into an icon of a hand making a very rude gesture. Ned swore, and hit the SatNav with his map. It fell from its mounting point, bounced off the radio, and landed heavily on the floor. Ned sighed, and picked it up.

"What did you do that for?" demanded the SatNav. "For one horrible moment, I thought that we were still in Wales!" There was a pause whilst the GPS repositioned. "Oh, we are. Why?"

"Our Quest is not yet fulfilled," intoned Ned.

"Oh very nice. That's dangerous talk, that is. You know that my new PPP function is still enabled? Well, it's prophesying trouble ahead. Storm clouds are gathering, mark my words!"

The junior wizard examined the bright blue sky. "Where?"

"Look, you don't have to see them yet. But they lie ahead."

"Yeah?"

"Yes. PPP tells me."

The CD player stuttered into life playing *It ain't necessarily so*.

"Appropriate" muttered Ned.

"You choose not to heed the warning?" asked the SatNav, in what the assistant assistant considered unnecessarily doom-laden tones.

Ned pursed his lips, examined his fingernails and watch, and then nodded. "Shut up and just keep a check on our position," he instructed.

The SatNav snorted. "That's just a basic function. I do that all the time anyway."

"Then why do yer keep giving us the wrong directions?"

"The directions are perfect. It's just reality that's prone to errors."

"Whose reality?" asked the junior wizard.

"Yours," sneered the SatNav. "I am designed to be perfect."

This blatantly insane comment brought forth gales of laughter from the Dark Wizards. The SatNav sniffed, and went back into standby mode to sulk.

"Right!" said Ned, "Has anyone any idea where we are?"

"That's what the SatNav is for," grumbled the assistant assistant.

"I'm not sure I trust it even to do that. I've been looking at the manual, and it were programmed by the French."

"Ah," agreed the junior, "then the source code is untrustworthy."

"What sauce?" asked the assistant assistant, who hadn't really been listening, as he negotiated a series of roundabouts, "I prefer brown sauce really. Does that go with SatNavs?"

"You what?"

"Well I always put brown sauce on chips, and they have chips inside them don't they?"

"The SatNav chips are silicon," sighed Ned.

"That's like sand, yes? So sort of like chips on the beach, then?"

"NO!" yelled the SatNav, stung out of sulk mode by the barbed comment.

"Funny, I always seem to get sand on me chips on the beach, too," agreed the junior from the back seat.

"My chip is not made of sand," insisted the SatNav. "And no one is to squirt brown sauce into my input socket."

"Ketchup?"*

*[Diversity in action. Right?]

"No!"

"Oh all right," smirked the junior. "Boss?"

"What?"

"All this talk of chips has made me hungry."

Ned thought for a moment. "OK, we'll stop at the next café."

The assistant assistant was surprised. "I thought that I were following The Banned?"

"We are. But THIS time, I know where they are going, so we don't need ter be watching them too closely."

"Here, on the left," called the junior, and the assistant assistant duly indicated right to confuse all the local traffic (as specified on his taxi drivers' instruction course) and pulled over into the car park on the left. The three Dark Wizards left the hearse, and walked purposefully towards the catering van parked in one corner. The scent of fried onions filled the air.

"How do we know where they are going, then?" asked the assistant

assistant.

"Well, we know that they've got The Sleigh on that trailer. Right?" asked Ned.

"Well, possibly right," said the junior.

"Why only possibly?" asked Ned, who was quite certain.

"Well, I've been reading this book," said the junior, a statement that was received with a measure of simple disbelief by his compatriots. "No, don't look at me like that, I have."

"What were it about?"

"It were a historical book, all about time. It said it was short, but it takes forever to read it, really. Anyway, him what wrote it was saying that everything is possible, all at the same time. So I were wondering, is it only possible that they've got The Sleigh?"

Ned looked at his junior very strangely. "So, if I tried to thump some sense into you, it's possible I might succeed?"

"Yes. No. Ow. And possible yer might not, too. Ow."

Ned nodded, shaking his hand. That somehow seemed more likely.

"Yer know the saying that a little knowledge is dangerous?" Ned grumbled, as the assistant assistant helped the junior wizard to get up.

"Wow, Bill," exclaimed the assistant assistant to the junior, "that makes you dangerous then, I suppose."

"I hadn't thought of it like that." The junior stood taller, and swaggered a little. "Bad, and dangerous to know. I like it." He walked deliberately across the rest of the car park, exhibiting a certain nonchalance in his walk.

"Here," said the owner of the catering trailer as he approached, "if you're walking like that because you've got something infectious, keep away. I've got enough trouble keeping my license as it is, without having diseased customers parading up and down. The Council will think that there's something wrong with the burgers again."

"Again?" asked Ned, suspiciously.

"Aye, well, there was that incident when they accused me of having that Diseased Mad Cow."

"Did you?"

"Yes, but I'm divorced now, so she doesn't come round here anymore."

"I'll just have the chips," decided the junior.

Ned sighed. "Look, it could be quite late before we eat again, so have a burger as well."

The junior looked mutinous for a moment, then cheered up. "Fried egg sandwich, with chips, that'll do me."

Ned sighed again, and turned to the approximate chef. "Egg buttie and chips three times, with coffee, please."

"Right you are, coming up."

Somewhere urban myth has it, there exists a roadside catering trailer selling perfectly cooked chips, succulent burgers and sausages, and golden fried eggs. Inevitably, it wasn't this one. Back in the hearse the wizards examined their food carefully, in case it was still capable of movement.

The junior bit into his egg, and then spent a few moments

searching the floor of the hearse, looking for his false tooth, propelled there by the rubbery consistency of the egg. Winding down the window, he muttered and the tyres of the catering trailer burst into flames.

"I said that was down to me to do," said Ned, mildly.

"I was provoked by this egg, Ned."

"I can tell."

All three watched with interest as the approximate chef tried, unsuccessfully to put the flames out with first the tea urn, then a small bottle of mineral water, and finally the cooking oil. The column of smoke rose lazily into the air, followed by the chef as one of the gas cylinders powering the burners exploded. Further explosions followed, as the cans of cola overheated. The return, approximately, of the chef to terra firma was greeted with applause. The approach of the chef, as he smoked, steamed and fumed, was greeted with less nonchalance, and the hearse duly pulled out of the car park with several sharp cooking knifes embedded in the back door.

"Right," said Ned. The assistant assistant indicated. "No, I meant turn left!"

"Right," replied the assistant assistant, complying. "So, where are we going, then?"

"Just keep going South for a while, I'll tell you when we turn off."

"Yes, but where are we going?"

"Well, those idiots have managed to damage The Sleigh, otherwise it wouldn't be on the back of the trailer. Right?"

"Here?"

"No, I mean you agree with me. And/or understand?"

"Yes, Ned."

"So, they have ter get it repaired, right?"

"Here?"

"No! I mean repaired at the special place Santa Himself goes to ter get it maintained," explained Ned.

"Right!" The driver indicated his intention to turn.

"No, not yet," sighed Ned.

"No, I meant I were following you."

"I thought we were following *them*?" asked the junior, as the hearse swept past a pub, whose car park was not entirely empty, containing as it did, a certain Mercedes Sprinter minibus with a trailer.

"No need," said Ned comfortably. "At the next roundabout, turn left."

"It's my function to give the directions," sulked the SatNav.

"But you always get us lost," complained the assistant assistant.

"Maybe, but at least I do it in a proper professional fashion. Can't trust amateurs, you know."

"Yer mean we should trust *you*?"

The SatNav sniffed, loudly. "Why not?"

The wizards all exchanged glances, then the assistant assistant made the appropriate turn onto a new road.

"I was about to suggest that," mumbled the SatNav. "So, where are we going then?"

"Somewhere secret," replied Ned.

"Well?" demanded the SatNav. "I can keep a secret!"

"So can I."

A screed of words flashed across the SatNav's screen.

"What did it say?" asked the junior, who hadn't been able to read them from the backseat.

"Nothing important," replied Ned who hadn't bothered to read the words, assuming that they would be rude and abusive, and largely unintelligible. He was right as it was a section from the user manual.

The assistant assistant was quiet. The workload in guiding the large hearse round the sharp bends as they drove deep into Snowdonia required all his concentration.

"Slow down, it's not a race, yer know," ordered Ned, as the large boxes in the rear of the hearse slid about alarmingly.

"Dead right," muttered the junior who didn't fancy another interview with the vampire presently asleep in the rear.

The assistant assistant slowed down a little, and executed a neat power slide around the next bend, which drew screams from the rear seat and from the SatNav.

"My PPP is going berserk!" the SatNav shouted.

"So?"

"It says that we are going to probably crash and possibly burn!"

"Is that one of them Schroedinger's Cat things?" asked the junior.

"I thought that it was that Principle of Heisenberg," suggested Ned.

"Is that the head of a posh school?" asked the junior, as the assistant assistant went around the next bend on two wheels, his long dormant rally driving skills being reborn after years of driving an arthritic taxi around town centers.

"No," replied Ned, inadvertently banging his head on the window. "Will you slow down?"

"Er, I can't, Ned."

"Why ever not?"

"The accelerator pedal has jammed. Still, we've come ter a straight bit now."

"NO WE HAVEN'T!" screamed the SatNav.

"Can't you change gear? Downwards?" asked Ned.

"I've tried, but it's an automatic, and nothing's responding."

"Why not turn off the engine?" called the junior, wrapping as many seat belts around himself as he could.

"Don't be stupid. Yes, the engine would stop, but I'd loose the power steering!"

The hearse, tyres squealing, slid around another hairpin bend with the occupants (including the SatNav) shrieking in perfect harmony with the tyres.

"I promised my mother I'd die peacefully, like me brother did!" howled the junior, as one of the large wooden boxes bounced painfully off the back of his head.

"Not screaming like his passengers, then?" asked Ned, acidly.

"Is there a straight bit coming anytime?" the assistant assistant asked the SatNav.

"Oh, I'm some use now am I?" asked the SatNav.

"Depends if there's a straight bit coming or not."

The rear of the hearse skidded again, and bounced off a tree that had inconsiderately grown a mere four feet from the verge of the road.

"Are you insured?" asked the junior.

[The reply was unprintable, and has therefore been removed from the text by the publisher, and the author duly admonished for permitting such language.] [Like I had anything to do with it – the author]

"Look, we are in Snowdonia," explained the SatNav. "Where there aren't any mountains, they have hills. When the supply of hills ran out, they planted lakes instead, and when the supply of lakes dried up, so to speak, they planted trees. The chances of a fairly straight bit of road are minimal."

The assistant assistant stamped his foot on the accelerator several times, but the pedal just flopped about loosely.

"This is strange," he panted, hauling again on the steering wheel and narrowly missing an oil tanker on a left hand bend, "we aren't getting any faster."

"What do you mean?" asked the junior, who still had an image of the tanker's rear wheels imprinted on his retina, from the near miss.

"Well, if the accelerator were jammed on full, we'd just keep getting faster until we reached the top speed of the car – van – hearse. But we aren't. We're stuck at fifty. I can keep us on the road – just – but can't change the speed. It's like a kind of magic."

"Magic?" asked the junior wizard, suspiciously.

"Magic?" demanded Ned.

"*Magic?*" screamed the SatNav. "It's them, I can feel it. That's what the PPP function was trying to tell me. I'm doomed, doomed, *doomed!*"

"Has anyone any idea at all what it's going on about?" asked Ned.

The assistant assistant shook his head. Ned sighed, flexed his fingers, and tried a brief counter spell. There was a bang and a flash, and he frantically sucked his fingers that had been momentarily set alight by the backlash.

"Wah!" he exclaimed.

"WWWAAHHHH" exclaimed the SatNav.

"WWWAAAHHH" shouted the junior, as the rear of the hearse again slid wildly across the road, the assistant assistant grimly fighting for control as the farside verge, complete with a substantial drop to a raging torrent below, slid in and out of his vision.

"Bet you wish you had a camera," Ned told him.

"Somehow, I don't think I'll forget that picture. Especially at three in the morning."

"So, that didn't work," the assistant assistant muttered.

"No," agreed Ned. "Let's try this one." He spread both hands over the gearbox, his fingers splayed out, and started muttering under his breath. The atmosphere inside the car grew cold, and the assistant assistant frantically switched the heater to demist, to keep the windscreen clear as he fought the juddering steering wheel. A light mist formed over the gearbox, and the hearse began to slow down. The junior and the SatNav sighed in relief, and when the speed fell under forty miles an hour, the assistant assistant relaxed too.

"How much longer on this road?" demanded Ned.

"Oh, navigating again am I now?" asked the SatNav.

"Shut up and tell me!"

"How very articulate. Did I show you the section in the manual dealing with disorganised and conflicting instructions? And the damage they can cause?"

"Never mind that," panted Ned. "We're under a magical attack, all right. Someone's trying to take over the control of the hearse, but I'm holding them off. Anyone give me a hand?"

"You've got two already. You only have two arms. Why do yer want another hand?" asked the junior, suspiciously

"No, put some of your power in here too, yer idiot!"

"Oh, sorry, what do I do?"

"Hands outstretched, fingers splayed out. Now open yer mind, that won't take you long."

"Oh, thank you. Wow, I can feel something. It's like, like, something eldritch is sucking all the stuffing out of me."

"Don't talk, just keep feeding the power in," ordered Ned. "Now, how much longer are we in these mountains?"

"At this speed, about twenty minutes, with one turn off to the south to the place I think you want to go to. If you take your hands away from the gearbox, about forever," replied the SatNav.

"Why forever if we're going faster?"

"Because my PPP says we'll be off the road in half a mile…near a stone…circle…*Druids!!*"

"Druids?" asked Ned.

"Yes," screeched the SatNav. "We must be under attack from druids. I'm so dead."

"Didn't know you were alive to begin with," said the junior, perplexed.

"I thought it were just a computer," agreed the assistant assistant.

"Just a computer? You think computers have voices like mine?" purred the SatNav.

Ned shuddered. The voice was uncannily like that of The Grey Mage's dragon receptionist.

"Ned," whispered the assistant assistant, "the speed's building up again."

"We must be getting closer to them," Ned replied. "It's getting too hard ter fight the power surges."

"There is a nearly straight bit of road just ahead," cried the SatNav, urgently.

"Right," said Ned. "When we get onto it, turn the engine off."

"Ned, how do I do that? We stole this remember?"

"Oh, sorry." Ned looked worried.

As the hearse weaved unsteadily, like a drunken politician, onto the nearly straight road section Ned lifted one hand from the gearbox, and placed it on the steering wheel. The lights on the dashboard died, but the engine bellowed as more power drove into the gearbox.

The assistant assistant bellowed as the hearse drove into the next bend.

Ned bellowed as he realised that he had just magically reengaged the steering lock, a fact discovered a moment before by the driver.

The SatNav bellowed as the hearse crashed through the long grass of the verge.

The junior bellowed as they crashed through the tall hedge beyond the verge.

They all fell silent, as the hearse momentarily became airborne, but all became very vocal indeed as it landed in a green but rather soft meadow, sank up to the axles in mud and stopped extremely quickly.

"Is everyone all right?" asked Ned after a moment. The assistant assistant groaned, the SatNav whimpered in fear. From the rear was an ominous silence. Ned slowly turned, to be greeted by the spectacle of the four wooden boxes, splintered open, in a heap. Lying flat on the back seat, and therefore (mostly) underneath them, was a very unconscious junior wizard.

"I say, I say!" called a voice back from the road. "Is anyone hurt?"

"Not yet," groaned the SatNav, "but it's only a matter of time."

Ned slowly climbed out of his door, and looked around. The hearse was about four feet away from, and about three feet below, the hedge that lined the road. "Why is it that we keep crashing through hedges?" he asked, plaintively.

"Look," the assistant assistant replied, "we tried telling you not to be so rude about the author at the Christmas party last year. Someone probably grassed you up to him."

"Who would do a thing like that?" wondered Ned.

They both turned to look at the junior, who had been knocked unconscious in the crash.

"Probably not," agreed Ned. "Someone else."

"Well, we are evil wizards. It's probably in someone's job specification."

"What," asked Ned, " spike the drinks, put mustard in the mashed potatoes, snitch to the author on what we are doing when he's not around?"

"I say, are you chaps all right?" puffed the old-looking gentleman, arriving slowly at the crash site, his fellows gamely bringing up the rear.

"I reckon so, thanks," said Ned. "Me mate here has gone to sleep, though."

The oldish gentleman peered vaguely at the junior.

"Oh, he'll be OK, I think. I say, we are most terribly sorry, chaps!"

"Weren't you fault," the assistant assistant said.

"Well, it was really, you see, we wanted you to crash into the field over there instead of here, then you wouldn't have had to walk so far."

"You what?" asked the assistant assistant.

The SatNav gave a long moan of dread, and Ned rapidly pulled it from the dashboard and dropped it into his pocket.

"Well, we had enchanted your vehicle so that you would crash into that field over there. So much easier for all concerned."

"You were making us crash?" Ned's tone dropped, and took on an air of menace.

"Oh yes, old boy. Sorry and all that, but well, you know how it is."

"You should be aware, we are from Caer Surdin, and not to be trifled with."

"Trifle?" asked the junior wizard, slowly waking up. "Can't stand trifle."

Five elderly, well-dressed gentlemen had now sidled into the field, and taken up station around the hearse. "Come on now, we've said sorry. How can we help? Can we offer you some refreshments? Roast Pork, perhaps? Chicken, or goose?"

"Well I am a bit peckish after that experience," agreed the assistant assistant.

"We'll take nothing from you," said Ned firmly.

"Oh dear, we had so hoped to avoid any unpleasantness."

"Then just go away," Ned replied. "Better yet, go away and find us a tractor."

"Well, we have a tractor, just over there."

"Where?"

"There."

"Where?" asked an unseeing Ned.

"There! But, none of us can drive it."

"We'll see if we can," said Ned, and led the way out of the field and across the road.

The field opposite did indeed hold the tractor, and also a small stone circle and forty oldish men dressed in white robes, who smiled in a welcoming fashion as they closed in on the trio.

Chapter Eight

"Right," said Ned, "so who are you lot, then?"

"Well, that's a bit of a problem really," the nearest replied. "You see, we've never been too good at coming up with acronyms."

"I thought that they were something builders have?" asked the junior.

"No, that's acroprops. We have a few of them too, but that's not what I meant."

Ned decided it was time to state their own acronym, to prop up his confidence. "Know that we are members of a Caer Surdin coven," he announced.

"I thought we were supposed ter keep that quiet, like?" hissed the assistant assistant.

"There's a time and a place for everything," Ned hissed back, not taking his eyes away the nearest white robed gentleman. Nor away from the large curved knife he was nonchalantly swinging in one hand.

"That's what that book I was telling you about were saying, too," agreed the junior wizard.

"Caer Surdin, eh? Well, we are – what is it this week, chaps?"

"WHOD, I think."

"Whod?" asked Ned.

"I thought that it was HOWDI, myself," suggested a second old gentleman, coming a little closer. The twinkle in his kindly eyes was matched by the flashes of light reflecting from the curved knife he just happened to be holding in a non-threatening manner.

"Howdi?"

"And whatever *he* likes to think, it is never going to be WIDDLE again. Ever." The speaker turned to Ned, and threw his arms wide appealingly, neatly decapitating a passing moth as he did so, and just missing Ned's throat with his blade.

"Can you imagine? Going to a conference of your professional fellows, associates and friends and having them announce 'And now we will hear from the WIDDLE representative?' I mean, honestly."

"What do they all mean?" asked Ned, as the three wizards continued to be urged gently towards either the tractor or the stone circle.

"Well, WHOD is the Welsh Hermetic Order of Druids. HOWDI is the Hermetic Order of Welsh Druidical Initiates."

"And WIDDLE?"

"We don't talk about that one. It's a bit Lunatic Fringe for me. Why are you bouncing about like that? Are you unwell?"

Ned clapped a hand over his pocket. The SatNav was vibrating urgently, never a good sign.

"Druids, then, I've always wanted to meet a druid," smiled the junior.

Ned, who had met several in The Grey Mage's accountancy practice, said nothing.

"We are sorry if we scared you at all, but we needed some extra bodies for the ceremony," explained the Chief Druid.

The three wizards drew a little closer together, and the junior changed his mind about his desire to meet druids. At least, not in their natural habitat.

"No need to be alarmed, lads. We and the chaps here have no desire to harm you at all."

The assistant assistant released the breath he hadn't realised that he was holding. Ned relaxed, and the SatNav vibrated with increasing urgency.

"What we'll do is this – offer you a bit of our hospitality, and, since we feel a bit guilty about it, Charles over there will get on the tractor and pull your van – it is unusually long, isn't it? – out of the field and back onto the road."

"That's good of you," replied Ned, cautiously. The SatNav was worrying him, as the vibrations were now coming in a repeated sequence of bursts. Three long ones, three short ones, three long ones. It reminded him of something he had learned once, long ago. Now what was it?

The Chief Druid led them into a small hut, where a table was laid with various snacks and a large pot of tea. "I'll just leave you here, and sort Charles out. See you in a moment," he said, and walked out of the hut.

"Great! Just what I could do with after that," sighed the assistant assistant, and reached for the food.

"Bide a moment," instructed Ned. "I'm not happy."

"You never are, though are you?" asked the junior, reaching for the teapot.

"Wait!" insisted Ned, and pulled the vibrating SatNav out of his pocket. Even without a power source, words sped across the screen, and then when Ned shook the device violently and banged it twice on the table, the words slowed down enough to be read.

Ned read them out. "You are in," his voice dropped. "Try being quiet you stupid git." He banged the SatNav on the table again.

"Are you alright in there, chaps? Need anything?" called a jovial voice from outside.

"Ah, er, we're fine, thanks," Ned called back. He beckoned the other two close, and showed them the words moving slowly across the screen.

'You – and me – are in great danger' spelt out the SatNav. 'These are druids. They will want to sacrifice all four of us in their ceremony.'

The junior held up four fingers.

Ned pointed at each of them in turn, then at the SatNav. He held up four fingers. The assistant assistant held up just two fingers, and ran for the doorway. He stopped as the doorway was filled by a white-robed figure. And again by the enormous curved knife at his side.

"Now, now, there's no need for haste. Please do try our hospitality whilst we recover your vehicle," ordered the druid.

The assistant assistant backed into the hut, and the doorway was filled by a door. Closing, firmly. Ned looked at the SatNav again.

'PPP' read the screen. Ned said something unprintable.

'I warned you. Druids want sacrifices. We are all doomed,'

suggested the SatNav, unhelpfully even in writing.

"Right," said Ned. "When will their ceremony happen?"

'Either at sunrise...'

"We've missed that one."

'Or sunset...'

"It's summer. What time is sunset?" asked the junior.

"The days are getting longer," mused Ned.

"Good!" said the junior, fervently.

"Probably three or four hours," the assistant assistant said gloomily.

"If they've been stood around here, in the middle of nowhere, all day then they won't want ter hang around all night, will they?" asked the junior.

"So, we have until sunset to escape," said Ned grimly.

"Chaps? I say chaps. Is everyone tickety-boo then?" called out the Chief Druid, pulling back the door and entering the hut.

Ned quickly dropped the SatNav into his pocket.

"Just felt that it would be discourteous not to bring you boys up to speed," smiled the Chief Druid.

"That's good of yer," acknowledged Ned.

"As you will know, it is the Solstice in just over a week. We always have a big ceremony here then, and you chaps are our designated guests of honour."

"Do you mean you plan to kill us?" demanded Ned.

"Good Lord no!" The Chief Druid looked very shocked. "We have a major ceremony taking place, we couldn't possibly defile that by killing you."

The assistant assistant looked terribly relieved, and the Chief Druid smiled benignly at him.

"I assure you that you will all die a natural death. After we have offered your still beating hearts to the Sun God to ensure prosperity for the New Year, death follows naturally. And may I say that I hope that you lot will do a better job than the last sacrifice? We tried a couple of Merchant Bankers and a Politician, and look what has happened to the economy as a consequence."

The junior gulped, and Ned started a magical attack on the Chief Druid. But the Druid just smiled, and the collection of hexes all turned into small bluebirds and started orbiting the Chief Druid's head. He smiled again, benignly. "Does you good to get close to nature, you know. Try it sometime – in your next incarnation."

He walked to the door, and turned back. "One more thing. We are not cruel or inhuman, so time will pass quite quickly for you, here inside this hut. Like the effect in that Fairy Hill near here."

"Is that all you have to say?" demanded Ned. The Chief Druid looked bemused, then smiled and pulled a pair of sunglasses on. He peered through the darkened hut towards the three wizards.

"I'll be back."

"He doesn't look like Arnie," complained the assistant assistant.

"But he does think he's a Terminator," the junior told him.

"I so wish you hadn't said that. Ned, you're the boss, how do we get out of this one?"

"I'm thinking about it," said Ned, and sat down at the table.

The junior reached for some food, but Ned knocked his hand away. "Are you daft? Don't touch it."

"Why, Ned?"

"You heard what the man said. This hut is enchanted, like a fairy hill. Touch that food or drink, and you'll wake up in a week tied ter a stone. Now, let me think."

"Can we get in touch with The Grey Mage? See if he can get us out?"

"Nah, he'd leave us to it," said the junior gloomily. "On the grounds that if we're daft enough to get caught like this, we should be daft enough ter get ourselves out."

"Could we plead insanity?" asked the assistant assistant, hopefully.

"Won't work," said Ned regretfully. "Druids all have a bit of madness in them anyway."

Ned stood up, and slowly walked all around the hut, paying particular attention to one corner.

"Right," said Ned. "That corner there, I don't think that they did the spells properly, and we stand a chance this evening of breaking out."

"Why wait?"

"Well, if we wait until the evening, they might not see us run across the field and grab the vehicle."

"Ah. Right. I see now."

"So, what are we going to do whilst we wait?" asked the junior.

"Tell some stories? Like the Arabian Nights?" suggested the assistant assistant.

"No way that's true! I don't believe it!" exclaimed Ned.

"Oh, I dunno," demurred the assistant assistant. "Stranger things than that have happened in the back of me taxi."

"Stranger maybe, but that was disgusting."

"Well, if you are going to take the umbrella's point of view, maybe," the assistant assistant agreed reluctantly. The junior wizard smirked.

"Is it getting dark yet?" asked the junior.

"Well, darkish, maybe. Let's see what the SatNav has to say." Ned pulled the SatNav out of his pocket, and looked hard at the screen. "Blast! It's frozen."

"Probably in terror," mattered the junior, who felt the same way.

"Look, I've get you out of tighter spots than this," said Ned with a confidence that he didn't quite feel.

"If you are talking about that time last year, when we got caught by the market traders association, that one were an easy fix," objected the junior.

"True," agreed the assistant assistant. "You bribed them with my bank card."

"And that time we were breaking inter Grizelda's house by the lake?" demanded Ned.

"You didn't get us out. She let us go."

"Shows that there is some good in her, then," agreed the junior.

"Which is probably why we can't recruit her," concurred Ned.

"Could do with her here now," muttered the junior, rebelliously.

"Come on lads, give me a chance. Now then, this corner over here." Ned sat by the corner he felt was less well controlled by the druids' spells, and after a moment started chanting, his eyes closed and his hands extended.

"Well?" demanded the junior after a moment. He was starting to lose confidence in his superior.

"Look, the author is trying to keep the suspense going so shut up, right? Maybe he'll let us out." Ned carried on chanting. After a moment, a dark hole appeared in the ground.

"What now? Do we have to crawl into that?"

"No, I just thought that we needed a toilet facility!"

The assistant assistant recoiled sharply, and Ned sighed, deeply, in despair.

"Right!" said Ned. "Our Great Escape!"

"So," said the junior, "which of us is Him?"

"Him?"

"Yeah, you know, him with the motorbike and the sunglasses."

"Steve McQueen," said the assistant assistant. "But we don't have a motorbike."

"Got the hearse."

"Wouldn't be the same. Trust me on this."

"Look, are we going out this way, or not?" demanded Ned.

They all looked at the hole. As they did so, a shining white light filled the hole, then departed, taking the whole hole with it.

"Probably not, then," said Ned slowly.

"Don't blame you for trying, chaps, but keep the noise down eh?" called a voice from outside.

"Plan B then, is it?" suggested the junior to Ned, who just glared.

"I say, who's this then?" shouted the same voice, outside.

Then there came a lot of muffled sounds, and the odd scream. The three wizards moved close together, out of an ancient instinct, and turned slowly towards the doorway. With a crack, the door was pulled off the frame, and hurled away into the night. Dimly, they could see a figure outlined against the stars of the night sky.

"Come with me, if you want to live," it told them.

Chapter Nine

After a restorative cup of tea, Grizelda sat back on her chair in the caravan. It would not be dark for some time, so what should she do?

"I know", she muttered. "Better go and get the broomstick seen to. Them dwarfs were supposed ter have it fixed last time, but really it's no better."

She stood up, and the chair creaked in relief. Pausing only to grab her hat, and throw some food in the direction of the grazing reindeer, she grabbed the broomstick, kicked it into life, and headed for the dwarf mechanics' workshop.

The dilapidated workshop on the nondescript industrial estate looked much like any other rented industrial unit. Rubbish drifted in windswept piles around the rusting sides of the building. Pools of water collected outside and carried a suspicious floating oily scum, although the oily scum floating about inside the unit were themselves strangers to water. An aura of desolation and indolence floated over the roof. Only the stacks of empty pizza boxes and the small mountain of beer cans betrayed the fact that these occupiers were to a degree different to the other tenants on the estate. Or perhaps they didn't: it was that sort of a place.

The faded sign over the closed doors read: DWARFS R US and featured a cheerful, smiling dwarf carrying a spanner: a sight calculated to deceive customers and attract those Government Agencies trying to stop misleading advertisements. The doors were shut tight, to discourage customers, and similarly unwelcome visitors. The half starved dog tied loosely to the front of the entrance was mute testimony to the absence of Revenue Inspectors in those parts.

The wind howled mournfully, and a drizzle of rain tried, unsuccessfully, to avoid falling. Also unsuccessful at avoiding falling was Grizelda, whose broomstick again misfired in the critical landing phase. The oily scum lurking in the pond boiled in sudden terror at her arrival; and the dog broke its lead, and fled. Slowly, a pointed hat rose, like Venus, from the waves. Unlike Venus, the remainder of the witch following the hat was neither a little lacking in the clothing department, nor possessed of a sweet smile. What might pass on a dark night for seaweed was in profusion, however.

"Why would anyone leave a puddle that deep near the damn doors!" muttered Grizelda, and hopping on one foot she removed a substantial boot from the other. She turned the boot upside down, and swore at the stream of water that poured out. Replacing the boot, she strode up to the door, and knocked, well, booted the door until a small hatch opened in the door and a face appeared.

"We're closed for rivet Rivet RIVET" muttered the face through a beard. As frogs don't have beards, he became clean-shaven rather quickly. The witch tapped her foot a couple of times, but the cold water splashing around her ankles dissuaded her from continuing.

Inside the workshop, a common business conversation was taking place as the nominal supervisor slammed down the phone on a customer.

"Did you tell him that his cheque came back?" asked a nearby dwarf, putting a piece of pizza down on top of a pile of unpaid invoices.

"Yes."

"Well, what did he say?"

"So did the faults you said were fixed."

"Rivet, rivet!" complained the frog from behind the door. The supervisor sighed, and walked warily to the small hatch.

"May we help you, madam? And could you see your way clear to restoring our colleague here?"

"I'm not happy that I've had ter come back here," declared Grizelda.

There was a certain level of muttered agreement on the other side of the door.

"What seems to be the trouble?" asked the supervisor, elected unanimously for the position of customer care consultant by everyone else.

"Me broomstick. It keeps cutting out, and droppin' me from a height."

The dwarf decided not to comment that it hadn't chosen enough height to stop her being able to complain. Like three thousand feet.

"When does it happen most, madam?"

"Landing. And taking off. Sometimes when I'm cruising , too."

A mental image of the middle-aged witch cruising traumatised the assembled dwarfs, some of whom began to sidle towards the rear of the workshop unit. The supervisor spun round:

"Stay where you are, you lot!"

"But that's Grizelda the Witch, and she's in frog mood," replied one, dropping his spanner in fright.

"It's still lunchtime, and I haven't finished me pizza," another complained. The supervisor bowed at the witch, turned to his recalcitrant colleague and glared at him from a distance of almost two inches.

"Do you want to tell her that?"

"Rivet rivet rivet!" suggested the new frog hopping up and down anxiously.

A further dwarf – in appearance they were more or less interchangeable, and regular customers normally differentiated them by careful study of the pattern of ketchup stains on their overalls – opened one of his pockets and removed a small parcel of courage he had been saving for a rainy day. He then carefully opened the visitor's door, and considerately closed the bear trap that lay just inside, and pulled the barbed wire to one side to allow Grizelda to enter without snagging her clothing.

Snorting, Grizelda stepped carefully through the door, and looked around the inside of the workshop unit. Stands stood along one wall, each bearing a broomstick in various stages of repair. Several had been there long enough to acquire their own spider colonies. She thrust her broomstick towards the nearest dwarf.

"Take it!" she ordered. The dwarf stepped back, but Grizelda stepped forward, until he reluctantly accepted her offered broomstick. He looked vaguely surprised that it didn't try to bite him, and looked around for a repair stand. The witch nodded in triumph, then frowned when oil dripped onto her boot from the shadowed, shrouded shape that was lifted above her head on a ramp.

"What's that?" she demanded.

"Um, special job that, a bit hush-hush."

Grizelda snorted, and lifted a corner of the thick sacking. A gleaming black Sleigh runner appeared, and an anxious dwarf jumped forward. Grizelda glared at him, and lifted a little more of the cloth, before dropping it back down again. The dwarfs all relaxed.

"Whose is this then?" asked the witch.

"Notsanta's."

"I can see it's not Santa's, his is bright red."

"No, it's Notsanta's."

"Notsanta?" the witch cracked her finger joints, and the echoes ran all around the workshop, terrorising the spiders.

The supervisor looked all around, but mainly for effect, and then lowered his voice. As he was only four feet high to begin with, the witch had to lean forward to catch his words.

"You know how every force in the universe has an equal and opposite reaction?"

"Like Ying and Yang?" asked Grizelda, a bit nervous that the conversation was about to get technical.

"I thought they were American comedians?" asked one of the dwarfs.

"Nah, that's Cheech and Chong," replied another.

"I thought they were the Marx brothers?"

"Don't start on Marxist jokes, Karl will moan at you all afternoon."

Grizelda glared at them, and they shut up.

"Anyway," continued the supervisor, "Santa is a force. And that belongs to his Opposite. You don't want to meet Him on a dark night, I can tell you."

"Why?" demanded Grizelda, confident that she was the most dangerous entity in the area.

"Because everything He's got is jet black, and you can trip over Him and His gear."

"What is it He does, then?" asked Grizelda.

The supervisor shook his head. "You don't want to know."

"Yes I do."

The supervisor looked around again.

"You know that Santa has a list of who's naughty or nice?"

Grizelda nodded.

"Well, Notsanta gets to visit all the girls who've been bad."

Grizelda's expression didn't change. "I thought that were Santa's job – and why he's always got a smile on his face," she said.

The supervisor leant forward and whispered a clarification in her ear.

"Ah. Right. OK, I'll keep out of His way then. If His vehicle is in here, where is He now, then?"

"Probably still in the pub," replied the nearest dwarf.

They all stepped carefully away from the silent, shrouded shape on the ramp. Oil dripped down, and smouldered on the concrete. Grizelda looked at her boot, but the oil had failed to make an impression there. She smirked slightly, and then turned her attention back to the supervisor.

"You told me that me it were properly fixed last time I were here with it."

"Well, we were sure it was, madam."

"Then why does it keep on misfiring?"

"Look, lady, the thing is so old you've got to expect problems. Why don't you buy a new one? You'd get a warranty and everything you know."

"It's not old. It's matured," objected Grizelda.

"Like a wine?"

"It certainly has a whine when it's running, that's true."

A second dwarf approached carefully. "I replaced all the bristles last time you were in here, madam. And the time before that we scarfed a new section inter the handle. But every time we put new bits in, the problems come back. I think you've got a virus."

Grizelda sneezed, and the dwarfs jumped back a pace. "I've had a head cold for a couple of weeks, it's true." She pulled out a handkerchief that, properly treated, could have replaced the research section of the government's biological warfare department for the next decade. After blowing her nose, she selfishly returned it to her pocket instead, to the general relief of the dwarfs.

"Not that sort of a virus. I meant in the operating system." The supervisor turned to his co-worker. "Have you run it through a spellchecker, Fred?"

"Did that last time."

"And?"

"That cheap new spellchecker you bought keeps defaulting to Chinese, and I think that the spells were coded in Beijing. It kept trying to order chicken fried rice and Peking Duck from the nearest takeaway."

"I see. Useless."

"Yes, because we've only got the pizza place and the fish n chip shop."

Grizelda started to draw a deep breath, then as the stale aromas hit her, changed her mind. "I'm going fer a cup of tea in the village. I'll be back in two hours, and I want it sorted out by the time I get back," she announced.

The dwarfs exchanged glances, and breathed a collective sigh of relief, as the door slammed behind her. One opened his mouth to speak, and four hands slammed across it in a reflex action. The door slid silently open, and the witch's head poked back in.

"Sorry, forgot something," she said innocently, then nodded at the frog at her feet. The reconstituted dwarf leant heavily against the wall, breathing hard, as Grizelda vanished outside.

The dwarfs looked at each other, and then at the offending broomstick. The lucky bearer of the broom held it gingerly, as though it might bite, and with relief popped it onto one of the special repair stands that stood nearby. The dwarfs clustered around it. One, with no regard for his personal safety, sucked his own teeth.

"Right!" said Fred. "We need some action, and we need some ideas."

"I've always got some ideas," called a fresh voice from the door.

"Oh no, not him as well," groaned he-who-had-been-frogged.

"Just what we didn't need," agreed the supervisor, putting his hand on his wallet in a protective fashion. "Dave, the spare part salesman. Who forgot to reset the bear trap, then?"

"Such a cheery welcome I always get here!" announced Dave, grunting slightly as he edged his big bag of samples past the barbed wire at the door. His grin, and flashing white teeth seemed to stand out brilliantly in the gloom of the workshop, as did the gold chain around his neck. The bracelets clinked solidly under the sleeves of his jacket.

"Who's going to offer me a cup of tea?" Dave demanded.

There was a pause, and then most of the dwarfs remembered that the kettle was at the back of the workshop, and all but the unfortunate supervisor shot off out of reach. The latter practised running on the spot for a moment, until he realised that Dave had a tight hold on his overalls, and couldn't escape with the others.

"This," Dave said with the manic cheerfulness taught to all high-pressure salesmen, "is your lucky day, chief!"

The dwarf looked dubious.

"I've got some samples I can let you have of some new potions for broomsticks, and some self spell restoring bristle lotion!"

"Oh yeah? Is it any better than the last lot you left us?"

"Why do you ask? It's new! It's got to be great!" enthused Dave

"Well, we used one of the last add-ons you tried on us."

"And?"

"The user complained. Said she flew round inverted for two days."

"So?"

"We had to buy her a new pointy hat. And some thermal underwear."

"You'll not have any trouble with this batch, I'll promise you. Look at what I've got here!"

Despite himself, and the noises from the back of the workshop where six dwarfs were fighting over who was going to fill the kettle, the supervisor looked into the open case. "What's that?" he asked, prodding a padded envelope. Dave maintained his fixed smile.

"The only free item there," he replied. "It's a service pack update for the Spellcheck Machine you leased last year. Fixes a couple of small glitches, you'll probably not even have come across them!"

"You mean the fact it defaults to mandarin?"

"The future's orange," Dave assured him. "I keep hearing that on the telly."

"No, mandarin the language," complained the dwarf.

"Oh that. Big market for us, China."

"All the tea cups you keep breaking."

Dave dismissed the criticism with an airy wave of an arm. The dwarf ducked, and winced as one of the heavy gold bracelets clanged off his once shiny mechanic's helmet. "Just put the disc in after I've gone, and all will be well. Now, let me show you this!"

Dave reached into his case, and reverently brought out a small glass bottle, and a large book.

"Latest thing! You dust some of this onto the bristles, and they get magically regenerated! The broom flies a bit faster, it's more economical, and the owner gets some extra kudos for being in tune with the environment."

"What's that book for?"

"Oh, that's the application manual, and the terms, conditions and exclusions. You don't need to worry about that!"

Wincing slightly from the weight, the dwarf picked up the tome from the floor, and flicked through it, squinting at the lettering. "It seems to be written in mandarin, too," he objected.

"Business is business, chief. It's the coming market, the business language for this century, and we all have be fluent in modern practice."

"This is a traditional business, though, this is."

"Well, I can see that," agreed Dave, looking around at the cobwebs growing over some customers' personal transport devices. He accepted the tea reluctantly offered by one of the returning dwarfs, and drank gingerly. With an extraordinary effort of will, he managed not to wince at the sugar level, and put the mug down on a nearby shelf.

"Try this!" Dave urged, grabbing a small box from his case.

"What is it?"

"In flight entertainment. Straps to the front of the broom."

A dwarf pressed a button on the box, and the workshop echoed to a strange, eerie noise. The dwarf pressed the button again, and silence returned. Dave spread his gleaming grin around for effect.

"Whalesong!" he announced. "Environmentally sound, too."

"Sound would drive me mental, right enough."

"What about this? Again straps to the broom, you can sell it as an add on when you use some of that dust on the bristles."

"What's it do?"

"Beeps loudly to tell you that a speed camera is close by."

Several dwarfs nodded with appreciation. "Then the rider can zap the camera, instead of the other way round," one approved.

"And," smirked Dave, "the 'piece de resistance'!"

"What is it resisting?" asked Fred.

"No, that's us, resisting buying it," the supervisor replied.

"Special new formula," Dave said in honeyed tones. "Go faster stripe paint. Paint this on the handle, you get an extra 20 mph until the paint wears off, and then you can sell a second application."

"How long does it last?"

"Depends how thick you apply it."

"You've got to be thick to apply it at all," protested Fred.

"It does what it says on the tin – jar – pot, though," Dave assured them. He pulled out his order pad. "I'll put you down for half a dozen, then shall I? A case of the bristle powder and some of the Traffic Alerts and a few pots of anti-drag stick polish."

One of the dwarfs had, quite fearlessly, stuck his head into the case to examine a packet that caught his eye. "Here, what's these red buttons in this box?" he asked.

Dave looked a little uncomfortable. "That was a demonstration line, but I'm not supposed to sell them now. They actually *did* work properly."

The dwarf mechanic's face registered disbelief. "What are they?"

"Emergency stop buttons. When pushed, the broom stops," Dave explained.

"What was the problem?"

"We had customers coming back, flying off the handle at us."

"Why?"

"The broom stopped so fast that they flew off the handle."

Dave went back to writing on his order pad, and placed some samples on the shelf beside the door. He looked again at the cup of (almost) tea, shuddered, and offered the supervisor his pad and a pen. Muttering in his beard, the dwarf signed the order form, ignoring as best he could the complaints coming from his wallet.

"I'll leave you these samples, see you next time." Dave waved genially to the dwarfs, and, his bracelets flashing, stepped back out past the barbed wire. A moment later, his wrist shot back in, grabbed his smile, and the door shut behind him. The dwarfs heaved a sigh of relief.

"Right," said Fred. He grabbed an armful of the new samples, and turned to glare at the offending broomstick. "What say we try some of this lot on it then?"

"Or all of them on it?"

"Good idea!"

The dwarf mechanics advanced on Grizelda's broomstick, which quivered on its stand as the weight of their glares fell upon it.

∗

The stand containing various assorted cakes quivered on the counter, until Grizelda withdrew her glare, and turned it onto the café owner instead.

"Tea!" she demanded.

"Yes, luv. Sugar on the counter, there."

Grizelda swept an imperious glance around the small room. Apart from one table, the place seemed empty. "You aren't very busy," she commented.

"No, luv." The café owner leant forwards across the counter. Grizelda leant forwards to meet him, and he recoiled quite quickly.

"It's that chap there. In the black cloak and hood. He keeps glaring at the folk who come in, and they leave quick."

"Won't work on *me*."

"Er, no, I can see that. I'll bring yer tea over, shall I?"

"And a couple of them scones."

Grizelda turned on her heel, and stomped noisily across the café floor to a table near the window. She looked out through the grime to enjoy the rain-washed vista, shuddered and turned back. The café owner approached with her tea and scones, and a pot of jam.

"Turned out nice again," he observed. Grizelda just looked at him, and he turned away.

"Two customers I get today," he muttered to himself, "and they are both miserable gits." The hood jerked slightly, and the café owner found himself lying on his floor, his nose embedded in a large sticky blob of ketchup. There was the suspicion of a snigger behind him, but the café owner ignored that and with enormous dignity – and a red nose- marched off.

"Pleased to make yer acquaintance," remarked Grizelda, conversationally.

"Do you know who I am, then?" asked the hooded figure.

Grizelda sipped her tea, and pulled a face. She tipped a large part of the sugar bowl into her cup, stirred it vigorously, and nodded in satisfaction.

"I saw yer – vehicle, let's say, in the workshop."

"Oh, right. I see. Does it not worry you?"

"Why should it? I'm not a child."

"In my official capacity, I can visit adults too."

"How is that? I thought that you only happened to children!" demanded Grizelda.

"I used to be a teacher, before I got the job of Notsanta instead of the pension. So, when the contract terms were being finalised I included School Inspectors in the target group too."

"Well I'm not one of them."

"Lucky for you," remarked Notsanta darkly, and with little regard for his personal safety, drank more tea.

"What were up with your sleigh then?" asked Grizelda, curious.

"Well, my reindeer aren't like the ones that red-dressed clown gets. His are usually friendly and approachable, at work anyway. Mine are more than likely to not just bite the hand that feeds them, but eat it up to the elbow as well. As a propulsion system, they are definitely outmoded and I keep trying to get an upgrade."

"Hum, I could see that. No traction control."

"Right. Anyway, purely out of spite I'm convinced, they keep kicking seven bells out of the sleigh runners, and messing with the onboard guidance system by peeing into the sensors. I mean, it was bad enough anyway, kept going the wrong way up one way streets, but when it has a 500 yard positioning error too: well you can imagine the complaints we got when kids were getting me instead of the other one."

"Humm, I could see that," agreed Grizelda.

"And when I visited some poor innocent lawyer:"

"Isn't that a contradiction in terms?"

"Probably. I mean, how was I to know he wasn't a School Inspector? He looked nasty enough to me. Still, the fuss he kicked up made them send the Notsleigh in for it's first proper service in years. Should be done soon."

Grizelda recalled the silent, shrouded and deserted shape on the ramp. "How long?" she wondered.

"Another three months, they tell me. That's three months I'm going to be sat in this café."

There came a chocked wail of despair from behind the counter, where the café owner was still engaged in a life or death struggle with the ketchup on his nose.

"Three months? I'll be ruined!"

"So will my insides be if I drink your tea for three months. Don't worry, I'll move on next week," sneered Notsanta.

The café owner subsided behind his counter, and looked at the small array of cleaning materials there. With a sigh, he dismissed them as useless, and picked up some sandpaper instead, and applied it to his nose.

Grizelda tried her tea again, pulled a face and put the cup down. "Nice meeting you, I think," she said to Notsanta, who nodded. Boots clumping on the floor, she left the café for the walk back to the garage.

"Oi!" called Notsanta as the door closed behind her. The café owner rose from behind the counter, with the sandpaper covering most of his face.

"More tea!"

"Right!" said Fred. "Just time to put this stuff on before she gets back!"

"Before who gets back?" asked Grizelda, quietly, into his ear.

Fred froze, which all things considered was possibly his safest course of action. Grizelda stepped back, then walked all around her broomstick, whilst the assembled dwarfs stood and watched her in horror. Or terror. Or both, for good measure.

"Am I a bit early, then?" she asked innocently. "Don't let me stop yer working."

"Right," said Fred, and as he watched in horror, the small paintbrush he was holding pulled his arm towards the broom, and started painting stripes along the handle. Grizelda nodded approvingly, and several of the dwarfs started to breath again.

"So" smiled Grizelda (no one was fooled by the smile, in fact several dwarfs started to edge away) "is it finished, then?"

"Well, madam" muttered the supervisor, "we've done all we can. If it don't work better this time, you really will have ter buy a new one."

"I see. Well, I suppose that if you really have done all that you can, I'd best take it for a test fly."

"Right," said Fred, again.

Grizelda held out her hand, and the broomstick slid from the repair stand into her grasp. Again, she nodded approvingly. "Whatever yer did to it, it feels better at the moment. No!" she held up a hand as a dwarf started to speak. "I'll find it all out for meself."

The witch carefully eased out of the door, and then took off slowly into the darkening sky. Behind her, the door slammed shut, and was quickly locked from the inside.

"Right!" said Fred, and started for the rear exit.

"Where are you going so fast?" called the supervisor after him.

"I'm going home. Now. Quick."

"Why?"

"Because Karl went and installed that Emergency Stop button, and I don't want to be here when she tests it out."

The remaining dwarfs looked slowly at each other, then at Karl. Then they all started running for the back exit.

Outside, over the lake, Grizelda's cloak streamed out behind her as she tried a power dive, followed by a sharp turn on pulling out of the dive over the shore of the lake.

"Wheeeeeee" she screamed in delight at the increased performance of her old broomstick. "Wheeeeeee" she screamed as her hands slipped on the newly polished stick. Twenty feet above the dark waters she sped across the lake, the go-faster paint stripes sparkling with power; the glossy finish of the wood improved by Dave's anti-drag polish, but a little slippery still in her hands.

"Now, I wonder what this red button here does?" she wondered. Out over the dark, cold, waters of the lake, she leant forward to try it out.

Chapter Ten

Back in the caravan, the still form of Count Notveryfarout stirred, and was suddenly fully awake, as vampires so often are. He lay still, testing the unfamiliar surroundings with all his senses, then gently lifted the bed that formed the lid of his makeshift sleeping box, and emerged.

Staggering over to the mirror, he reared backwards, appalled at the dusty vision before him. The Count sneezed, and shook out his clothing. The bedroom turned grey as the dust settled on every possible flat surface. He then delicately, with averted eyes, stepped over the pile of used clothes and made his way into the living area of the caravan.

"Is there anybody there?" he called.

A sneeze from underneath one bed reassured him that Hugo had survived the night, so the Count pulled the pile of laundry away from the box and lifting the lid released his fellow vampire from durance vile. And the vile laundry that had somehow joined Hugo in the under seat receptacle.

Hugo, incapable of speech for the moment, nodded his thanks. Together, they carefully lifted the seat on the other side of the caravan, and revealed a very pale Percival.

"Come on, stop malingering!" ordered the Count.

"Perhaps he isn't malingering this time," croaked Hugo.

"Don't be silly. He's a vampire, what can hurt him?"

"Well, you know how we all have this depression thing? Maybe he's done something, well, silly."

"You mean – Hari Kari?"

"What, Harry Carrie, the local butcher? What's he got to do with us?"

"No, you idiot! I mean he could have killed himself."

"Who, Percival? I don't think so, Count. If he tried to cut his own head off, he'd miss."

"Hum." Count Notveryfarout grabbed hold of Percival, Hugo helped, and the two lifted their friend out into the darkness of the caravan. They dropped Percival on the opposite seat, and Hugo pummelled a bit of afterlife back into him.

"Where are we?" asked Percival, opening his eyes. "I was having an awful dream, full of scary monsters."

The Count sniffed, derisively. "Percival, where's your self respect? Vampires should not have bad dreams!"

"I heard you telling Her one about this enormous trombone that chased you along a beach," muttered Percival.

"That's private. Besides, that dream's been in my family for years. My great-great-great-great grandfather invented it."

"Why, Count?"

"How would I know? Maybe he was a conductor, and hated trombone players."

"My father was a bus conductor. He hated trombone players too, when they got on his bus."

"An ORCHESTRA conductor, not a bus conductor," sniffed the Count. "Maybe his first meal as Vampire was a trombonist. I don't know. But I do know that nothing should scare us."

"That's right, Count!" agreed Hugo, looking menacing.

The door of the caravan flew back with a crash.

"AAAAHHHGGGHHHHHHHHH" screamed all three vampires, in terror.

There, in the doorway loomed a wild, fearsome figure of horror. Lightning flashed at its back, for dramatic effect and a small fee.

"AAAAHHHGGGHHHHHHHHH" screamed the vampires again.

The figure stepped into the caravan, and the vampires pressed back against the wall, then recognised a thoroughly soaked, dishevelled and furious Grizelda. The sound of thunder shook the caravan, but abated as Grizelda hauled her feet free of her drenched boots. A medium sized fish fell out of her dress and wriggled madly on the floor until she grabbed it, and dropped it into one water filled boot, where it lurked malignantly.

"Er, been fishing?" asked Hugo, nervously.

"No, I've been swimming. Which is what them mechanics will be doing when I catch up with them tomorrow," snarled Grizelda. The three vampires shuddered, and for a moment felt a passing sympathy for the targets of her wrath.

"Now you lot are up and about, I suppose you will be wanting a session each in a bit?" demanded Grizelda.

"Well," started the Count when it became obvious that neither of the other two vampires was about to say anything.

"Well, you will have to wait for a bit. I need ter get dry first. You, Hugo, you can put the kettle on for me. And one of yer can get rid of that fish." Grizelda stamped into the back bedroom and slammed the door, making the whole caravan rock. Water slopped out of the boots she had left on the floor, and the fish looked a little alarmed. Percival approached carefully, and shrank back as a tail shot out of the boot and slapped him across the face.

"Percival," decided the Count, "as you are the nearest, you can go and take that boot and the fish back to the lake. Hugo, you can make her a nice cup of tea."

"What are you going to do, then, Count?" asked Hugo.

"I," announced the Count, "will supervise."

Percival nodded gloomily. That was exactly the answer he had been expecting. There came a selection of strange noises from the bedroom, as Grizelda, grunting alarmingly, divested herself of her soaking wet garments. Suddenly, being out of the caravan didn't seem the worst available option to him, and he grabbed the boot and slipped out into the night.

Carefully closing the door to the caravan behind him, Percival discovered that he was face to face with a curious reindeer. Vampires are famed for their ability to control lesser creatures, but Santa's reindeer probably don't count as lesser creatures. The reindeer were convinced that they didn't, and Percival was sufficiently short of self-confidence to agree with them. Bunsen lowered his head threateningly. Percival tried a glare, which didn't work.

"Nice, er, reindeer," he tried, in the face of all the evidence. Bunsen pawed the ground with his front leg. Percival edged past onto the grass, keeping a firm grip on the boot and prepared to take off.

Burner trotted around the side of the caravan with his antlers down, and assisted the process. Screaming, Percival was tossed high over the top of the van, to the general amusement of the reindeer who watched smugly, only to feel disappointed as the vampire reached the top of the launch curve, and wobbled off into the night sky.

The Count looked out of the window, watching Percival soar rather unsteadily across the night sky towards the lake. "He's off to a flying start," he said approvingly. "Hugo, get the kettle on quick, before she comes out of there."

Hugo filled the kettle, and then carefully approached the somewhat erratic stove. "Have you seen her light this thing?" he asked.

"Yes, but she just glares at it until it lights up in fear," replied the Count.

"So, how am I meant to do it then?" asked Hugo.

"Well, you turn on the gas,"

"Gas? In these conditions? How can you tell if it's on? If we weren't vampires, I'd have been gassed in my sleep yesterday, I tell you."

"Sssshh!" hissed the Count urgently. "She'll hear you!"

They both stopped, and turned to look at the rear bedroom. After a moment, the sounds of industrial undressing resumed. Hugo approached the stove cautiously, then turned the gas tap to on and glared fiercely at the stove.

"Count, it isn't working!" he hissed as loudly as the gas flooding out into the caravan.

"Try a match," suggested the Count. Hugo selected a matchbox from the shelf beside the stove, and prepared to strike a match. As he did so, a ballistic, water filled boot flew across the interior of the caravan and took the matchbox out of his hand, before knocking him back onto a seat and landing in his lap. Hugo sat and stared in horror at the small lake, complete with assorted pond life, which covered his trousers.

"Are you after a quick second death then, you muppet?" demanded Grizelda.

"If yer had struck that match, then the explosion would have blown us all into the next life!" She strode across the caravan half dressed, and the Count covered his eyes in a gentlemanly fashion. Grizelda threw open a couple of windows to let the fresh night air into the caravan, and the smell of the gas out. She turned back, and waved vaguely at the stove, which fizzled sheepishly into life.

"All you have to manage now is the tea," she growled, and returned to the mysteries of dressing.

Hugo hopped across the room, and vanished out of the door. He returned a couple of moments later, just as the kettle boiled, with the strange, shuffling walk employed out of time by every man with soaking wet trousers. He turned round to see Grizelda, magically dressed in dry clothes, appear silently out of the bedroom. Without her enormous boots, he realised, she was capable of moving as quietly as any other predator.

"Er," he started.

Grizelda sighed, deeply. "You might be a vampire, but inside yer just a typical bloke, aren't you?" she asked, wearily. "Mostly completely useless, until it comes to something no one else with a second brain cell would want, and then you're brilliant."

"Now be fair, Grizelda," objected the Count. "When Hugo became vampire, tea hadn't been invented. How is he supposed to know how to make it?"

"It's tea, just how hard do yer think it is? You put some tea in the pot, add water, and bingo: a couple of minutes later you get tea."

"Sounds a bit technical," grumbled Hugo. "How do you know how much tea to put in the pot?"

Grizelda sighed again. "Everyone knows that, surely. One per person, and one per pot."

"One what?"

"Teaspoon of course."

Hugo nodded, and looked at the selection of spoons before him. No two were the same size, or indeed the same colour or shape. Grizelda grabbed one at random, spooned loads of tea into the teapot, glared at the kettle until it emptied itself into the teapot, and nodded in satisfaction.

"Now, I'm going ter sit down and have a nice cup of tea. After that, we'll start on our sessions; so you two gentleman go just go off and do whatever it is you need to do for half an hour. Then I want all three of you back here. Got it?"

Hugo nodded, and was out of the caravan in a flash. Count Notveryfarout followed more sedately.

"Funny," he muttered as he closed the door behind him. "I thought that as we hired her, we should be in charge."

Hugo looked at him as if he was mad, which of course he was – that was why he was having counselling in the first place.

"Let's just go and eat, find Percival, and come back as told," he suggested.

The Count nodded, and the two vampires rose into the air,

frustrating the efforts of the reindeer as they came galloping around different sides of the caravan, to meet with a mighty crash, two feet below their targets. The Count nodded again, this time in satisfaction, as Bunsen and Burner fell over, momentarily stunned by the impact of the collision.

Hugo gave the still bodies a very significant look, but the Count pulled him away.

"Don't be daft, Hugo," he said. "They belong to Himself. You'd be mad to drink from them."

"But I thought that we'd agreed that we are a bit mad anyway?"

"I might be mad, but I'm not stupid. And I don't want Santa after me."

The vampires merged into the gloom as they headed for the town.

Back inside the caravan, Grizelda picked up her cup of tea, and poured four large spoonfuls of sugar into it, before stirring vigorously. She took a sip, and leant back with a contented sigh. Before too long the pot was empty. She poured the last liquid in the cup into the sink, and upended the tealeaves that had collected in the bottom of the cup into the saucer. Carefully she studied the patterns in the leaves. But besides telling her that she would shortly be visiting the toilet, the saucer was full of secrets, which she couldn't read.

"There's something strange going on, I can sense it," she muttered to herself. "Mebbe it's to do with the Banned, wherever they are. Or mebbe not. But by the pricking of me thumbs, there's a bad moon rising."

She sighed, and examined the tealeaves again, before acknowledging the truth that *had* been revealed to her and heading for the bathroom. Whilst contemplating infinity, as represented by the efforts of a spider to scale a smooth wall, she also checked her broomstick and regulation hat that were stored in the conveniences for convenience. Satisfied that all her necessary professional equipment – except for her big boots – was in order, she emerged ready to meet the challenge posed by her attempt to cure the three vampires of their depression.

Grizelda stared around the caravan. She felt in the mood to give the vampires a hard time, and wasn't sure that the surroundings were conducive to her plans. She fussed around, arranging the table, clearing the dirty clothes away by dumping them into the underseat box used by Percival, removing the wilting flowers from the vase and throwing them out through the window (to be eaten with every sign of enjoyment by Bunsen) and cleaning the floor by shifting the rug over the worst stain. Housework done, she sat back with a sigh, to await her customers.

After some time, she shifted in annoyance, walked to the door and peered outside.

Nothing. "Where have the dozy beggars got to?" she muttered, and tried to read whatever message was in the stars. After deciding that it was rude or abusive rather than helpful, Grizelda decided that there was only one thing to do.

"Suppose that I'll have ter go and find them," she said to herself, and turned back inside. As she did so, there was a loud thump on the roof, and Percival bounced off and landed hard on the ground, the Count and Hugo alighting beside door with more grace.

"He's had a shock," explained Count Notveryfarout, glaring at Bunsen who was trotting towards the dazed Percival with a fixed stare.

"Is that so?" asked Grizelda. "What did he do, land on a cattle prod?"

"Close. He tried to drink from an electrician."

"What?"

"Exactly," agreed The Count, to Grizelda's bewilderment. "Too many watts. Or volts, or something. Anyway, it made his hair stand on end, so we thought that we'd better bring him back here. And look, he's still holding your boot!"

"At least it's nice and dry now," grumbled Grizelda retrieving her boot from the vampire's twitching hand, and shoving it beside its fellow under the table.

The three vampires exchanged guarded looks.

"Right!" said Grizelda. "I've got me tea, the mystic herbs have been scattered all around, and there's a box of rags there in case any of yer need a good blow. Who's first?"

Hugo and Percival took quiet steps backwards. The Count suddenly found himself elected, and with a sigh, sank down upon the appropriate chair. Hugo and Percival slipped out into the night. Grizelda smiled, something The Count found quite terrifying.

"So, where were we?" Grizelda reached into her bag, and pulled out a rather tattered black book. She riffled through the pages at some speed, and then leant backwards. The seat creaked alarmingly, and she promptly leant forward instead. The Count leant back further, and the legs on his chair slid forwards, depositing him neatly on the untidy floor.

"Stop making a mess," Grizelda said absently, still examining the pages of her book.

The Count pulled a face, and climbed back onto the chair.

"So, we were talking about yer depression," mused Grizelda.

"Remind me why you feel bad all the time."

The Count looked at her. "Look, you've had some experience now of the two other vampires I seem condemned to spend eternity with. Wouldn't you feel depressed?"

"So, would you say that you feel depressed because you lack the esteem of yer peer group?"

"Peer group? Peer group? Neither of them are nobles."

"Both have posh names," Grizelda pointed out.

"Those aren't their real names. They adopted them when the became Vampires."

"Oh. So, not your social equals, then? Do you lack company?"

"Look, I'm a Vampire. I sleep all day long, and only come out at night."

"Me niece is a bit like that, and she's not a vampire. At least, I'm sure that I would have noticed if she was."

The Count sighed. "She's a teenager I suppose. Imagine being stuck with a couple of teenagers for a hundred years, and you'll start to understand."

Grizelda pulled another book out from a pocket, and quickly flicked through it. "Are you worried about getting old, then?" she asked. "Do yer feel that time is passing you by?"

"For heaven's sake Grizelda, I'm three hundred years old. Of course time is passing me by. Look at that world out there. It's full of computers that no one understands, mobile phones that everyone owns but complain about all the time, and everyone is always in a hurry to be somewhere else. Science seems to be carried out on TV instead of in decent dungeons, and all the evil wizards have establishment jobs. How is any decent vampire supposed to cope with that lot?"

Grizelda was silent.

"I know that times change, and we have to change with them. That's part of being a vampire. But sometimes…" The Count fell silent.

Grizelda nodded sympathetically, and pushed the box of rags towards The Count. "Are there any compensations?" she asked.

The Count thought for a moment, then brightened. "Well, I never have to watch daytime TV."

"I see," said Grizelda (who didn't, but was following the instructions in her Guide For Counselling The Depressed). "What other things cheer you up?"

"Last time I went on a holiday. Without those two. I left them to fend for themselves, and had a week in Italy."

"And did you enjoy it?"

"Damn right I did! It made such a change to meet some elegant, interesting people for a change." The Count's eyes glittered for a moment as he sat up straight, licking his lips at the memories.

"And?"

"And then I had to come back here to a diet of welsh dwarfs and their B Negative blood. Is it any wonder that I'm depressed?"

Grizelda nodded sympathetically, and dozed off as The Count droned on with his litany of complaints. Then she blinked, and shook her head. "I'm sorry," she lied, "say that again?"

"I mean, just yesterday, do you know what I had for supper? A mechanic. And he was quite rude, too."

"There's no respect left, is there?" agreed Grizelda.

The Count nodded glumly. "All he could talk about was this secret job they had on."

"What were it?"

"He didn't tell me. It was a secret."

"I thought vampires were supposed to be able to get secrets from anyone?"

"In his case, I thought that the afterlife was too short."

Grizelda was wondering to herself if this was one of the dwarfs she had met recently. "What did you do with the dwarf?"

"We had a few drinks, and then I let him go. It's not done to kill the small ones, you know. Got to leave them to mature."

"He was a dwarf!"

"Still is, I expect."

"Yer know what I mean. He was probably nearly as old as you."

"Shame he didn't taste better then. You seem interested in him – do you know him?"

"I'm meant ter be asking the questions!"

"Sorry," apologised The Count, looking down.

"I reckon I know how to sort you out," asserted Grizelda. "I know the cure!"

The Count looked up again. "I've always liked their music. Can you get me an introduction?"

"No, just take a holiday twice a year."

"Do you think that will do the trick?"

Grizelda looked around, and whispered: "Having to hang around with that dozy pair would make anyone feel depressed. Give it a try, what have you got to lose?"

"You know, Grizelda, I think that you are quite right! I'll have a take-away from the Travel Agents tomorrow night!"

The Count walked out of the caravan with a spring in his step, allowing Hugo to shuffle in and take his place.

Grizelda sighed, and tried to look encouraging. "So, Hugo, how do we define your problems?"

Hugo looked back at her. "You've just had The Count in here, and you wonder why I've got issues?"

Chapter Eleven

The Sprinter negotiated a roundabout at a sedate pace, causing a few raised eyebrows. The Banned were used to a more lively driving style from their head roadie.

"Eddie? Why are yer going so slowly?" asked Haemar.

"Der."

"What did he say?" asked Jerry.

"The Sleigh is so heavy that he can't get the minibus to speed up like he normally does."

"All that? From Der?"

"It's just the way he said it," explained Haemar.

"Oh."

"Der."

"What did he say this time?"

"Der," repeated Eddie, helpfully. Jerry looked blank, and Haemar sighed.

"Eddie reckons that it's got ter be breakfast time."

Mungo, squashed between Felldyke and Scar, agreed.

"So, where are we going ter eat?" asked GG.

"I've been here before," offered Fred. "There's a pub not far up this road that does good breakfasts."

"Isn't it a bit early to go to a pub?" asked Boris.

Everyone else in the minibus turned to look at him, astonished.

"Well, isn't it?"

Haemar objected. "We're musicians, not alcoholics."

"There's a difference?"

"Der."

"Eddie's right. It can be hard to tell the difference," sighed Fungus.

"Anyway," put in GG, "alcoholics are anonymous, and everyone knows who we are."

Ahead, a long low building with a large car park appeared.

"That's it!" called Fred.

"Plenty of room to park," agreed Haemar.

"Der," agreed Eddie, and carefully swung into the empty car park. He backed the trailer under an overhanging tree, so that The Sleigh was not easily visible from the road.

"Right," yawned Fred, and climbed out of the minibus. He walked round to the back, and checked the coverings. Straightening up, he was just in time to see the door of the pub close behind Scar as The Banned and his colleagues headed in search of food.

Inside the pub, Haemar and Felldyke examined the menu. Then ordered most of it, several times. to the publican's evident delight. He was so pleased that he didn't say anything when Scar and GG started pulling tables together, and even agreed to turn the house music off entirely. Fungus pulled his sax from its covers, and started to warm it up.

"What's he going to do with that then?" the publican asked Haemar. Haemar didn't raise his head.

"Well?" demanded the publican.

"He might be going to use it as a straw, but I suspect he's going ter play it," replied Haemar. "Here, Felldyke, do you want some garlic bread too?"

Suddenly, the sound of the sax filled the bar. The few other patrons stopped eating, and the publican paused in the middle of pouring a pint. Fungus stood apart from the others, in a corner by a window. The last few hours after the gig hadn't drained the adrenaline from his system, and he felt like expressing himself. After a few moments, Haemar pulled his harmonica from a concealed pocket, and joined in the melody. Felldyke wandered across to an empty table, and started a quiet rhythm using just his hands on the tabletop. The world held a breath, and for a brief moment everyone felt clean, even without the benefit of showers.

Outside, with a snarl of exhaust, a long black van drove past. The publican realised that expensive beer was pouring away into the drain, shut his mouth with a snap and grabbed a fresh glass. The music still filled the bar, but the spell had broken. The other customers turned back and finished their meals.

"Wow," breathed Jerry when Fungus and Haemar finished, and paused for breath. "That was just amazing. Why don't you do that on stage?"

Fungus shrugged.

"Not enough market for it," Haemar said, still with a far-away look in his eyes. "That's why we had ter start playing Blues and Rock and Roll, instead. That's where the money is, these days."

"You get to do that and get paid as well?" asked Boris, in awe.

Scar looked strangely at him. "We're professionals. Being paid is what it's all about."

"Talking of that," Haemar said to Jerry, "Are we getting paid fer this gig then?"

"What gig?" asked Mungo.

"Look, we're supposed to be having a day or so off, then carry on with a few gigs."

"If we can find any," muttered Felldyke.

"See, we need ter record some songs for this album we're putting together," explained Haemar.

Mungo and Jerry exchanged glances. Then exchanged a long look. Then a stare. Then they nodded to each other.

"Tell you what," said Mungo, "you help us to get The Sleigh sorted, we'll sort you with the gig to end all gigs."

"Oh yeah? Where?"

"Santa's Grotto."

"I thought that Santa lived at the North Pole?" asked Felldyke.

Close to the window, Fungus took a long drink out of the nearest glass, and then picked up his sax again.

"Nah," Mungo said, raising his voice over the music, "it was too cold. The glue wouldn't set properly on anything we made out of wood so we went underground."

Felldyke nodded approvingly. Going underground rang a bell with him.

"So, we've got this big set of caves now. Loads of room, it's warmer, and there's less chance of a group of drunken explorers with a TV crew turning up when we're a bit busy."

Behind them, Fungus was improvising in a free-form way, whilst Haemar lay across a long bench close by, his eyes closed. Next to him, GG and Scar sat at a small table, talking quietly. Jerry, Fred and Boris sat at the next table, listening. The few other customers were also very quiet, as the sax filled the room with sound. Silently, at the far side of the room, the twin doors swung open, and closed. Slowly the music slowed and stopped. There was a crash, as a bass amp dropped heavily to the floor. Jerry stared open mouthed at the chubby red dragon carrying a bass guitar.

"Hi Guys, Surprise!"

GG looked up, unsurprised. "Hiya, Dai."

"What? You know him?" asked Jerry, as the dragon headed for the bar.

"Yeah, he's our bass player."

"You have a dragon for your bass player?"

"So? He stands his drinks round like the rest of us."

"Better than some," agreed Haemar, failing to look at Felldyke. Felldyke pulled his face anyway.

"What are you doing here anyway?" asked GG.

Dai looked confused, and raised his Bass. Then put the glass down and raised the guitar instead. "There's a gig soon isn't there?"

"I thought that you wouldn't come this far into North Wales?"

asked Scar.

"Bet it were another incident like that time in mid-Wales," Haemar said knowingly.

Dai looked sheepish. "Er, it was only one sheep, and I was peckish, see…" A chorus of groans greeted his confession. "So, I thought I'd make myself scarce for a bit, and I thought of you guys."

"Yes, but how did you find us?" asked GG.

"That was easy. I knew where last night's gig was, so I headed for that, and saw the Sprinter pull in here. So, I landed discreetly, and wandered over."

"Discreetly?" asked Jerry, confused. "How can a dragon fly in and land and be discreet?"

"By not falling over," Dai told him.

"And by getting the drinks in," suggested Haemar. Dai sighed, and nodded to the barman, before picking up the menu.

"I thought that you ate recently?"

"It was mutton dressed as lamb," explained Dai, and ordered a full cooked breakfast as the laden trays ordered by Haemar and Felldyke started to appear.

"So, what's going on then?" asked Dai, as the Banned settled down comfortably to eat and drink.

Fungus replied, but his mouthful of food rendered the content unintelligible, as well as indigestible. GG didn't look up from his plate, but just pushed the ketchup across the table anyway.

"Well," started Jerry, moving closer to Dai and then pushing his chair back again when he realised how warm the dragon was, "We were on our way to the gig, when we had an accident. Fungus and your mates here have agreed to help us out in getting the transport to a suitable garage."

"A bit like Roadside Recovery, only this one doesn't demand your credit card before getting out of the truck," added Mungo.

"Ah," said Dai. "So, when's the next gig, guys?"

There was a silence. Dai drank another large whisky, to help restore his fuel levels, and leant back. There was still a silence, as everyone turned to look at Fungus.

"Well, I hadn't actually confirmed that yet." Fungus buried his face in his drink. Haemar glared at him.

"You do realise that Adam is wanting some recordings, don't you? For an album? How are we going to do that if we don't play?"

"Something will turn up," Fungus said confidently. The Banned looked disbelievingly at him. "Look, I'll find us a gig, and Eddie can record it!"

"Der!"

"Eddie, it doesn't matter if you've never recorded a gig before."

"Der."

"Well, all right, look, everyone made bootleg tapes back then. That just means you've got experience. All you need to do is press the 'play' and 'record' switches at the same time on the console, just like one of them old tape recorders."

"Der."

"You'll be fine, stop complainin'."

Jerry pulled hard at one of his ears. This was a common sign that he'd had a brainwave, and had been known to make his colleagues hide behind the reindeer in the past.

"I've had an idea!" he announced.

Mungo groaned. "Another one?"

"Yes, but this one's brilliant!"

There was a significant lack of enthusiasm around the enlightened tables.*

*[The tables had not been granted spiritual enlightenment, but had been released from their earthly burden as the supply of food vanished. In the end, there's probably not much difference.]

"After we get the Sleigh sorted, we'll fly you all back to the Grotto, and you can do a gig there!" Jerry cried, excitedly.

"I just said that," grumbled Mungo.

"Think what we'll make on the ticketing alone!" hissed Jerry quietly to his fellows, but not too quietly for Haemar to fail to hear him.

"He's right there!" whispered Boris, and Haemar marked him down as a slippery customer, possibly with concert promoter's genes.

"What grotto?" asked Dai, further topping up his fuel level, and leaning backwards.

"Santa's Grotto."

Dai choked and coughed, and the resulting flames bounced off the ceiling, via the smoke detector.

"Here, you can't smoke inside here!" yelled the outraged publican, and flung his body across the bar to preserve the large stack of notes he was counting from the sprinkler system.

"Oh, sorry," replied Dai. GG dealt with the problem by climbing onto Scar, and closing the sprinkler system off with a large piece of chewing gum he'd found under his chair.

"Ooof" grumbled Scar, as GG jumped down.

"Right you lot, out!" demanded the publican.

"Yeah, it's time we got on anyway," said Haemar.

"Where are we going?" asked Dai.

"Tell you in the bus," replied Haemar.

"I'll tell yer this," grumbled Felldyke a few minutes later. "This bus ain't big enough."

The already rather full bus was now extremely full with the addition of a slightly drunken welsh dragon.

"Look, it's not too far," Fungus told them from the relative comfort of the front seat. Jerry was squashed in between Fungus and Haemar, and every time the bus lurched, his nose came into contact with the windscreen.

"Turn left here," he mumbled, and Eddie swung the Sprinter slowly around the corner. The chorus of complaints left him in no doubt however that his passengers were in discomfort.

"Der" he apologised.

"What's on the CD?" asked Fungus, to lighten the atmosphere. Haemar peered at the compilation case.

"*The Passenger* by Iggy Pop", he reported, and the barrage of complaints started again from the back. "Yes, I know," Haemar called, and reached for another CD.

The jazz compilation soothed the Banned, but perplexed the Little Helpers. However, there attempt to complain was quickly smothered when Dai stretched his wings a little, "Just to ease the cramp," he assured them. Lying half under a seat, and half under the dragon, Mungo implored his friends to keep quiet.

"He's a bit drunk," he hissed into what he hoped was Fred's ear. "If he has an accident, I'm toast!"

Fred turned to look at the problem. "As long as you like soggy toast," he agreed.

Mungo pulled a face as Boris twisted towards them. "It's a bit cramped in here!"

"You want to try being underneath a sleeping drummer. Why does he have to keep his drumsticks there?"

"Are you sure that they are his drumsticks?" asked Fred.

"Damn right I am! But the sooner we are off the bus with these crazy madmen, the better."

"It's the last time I listen to one of Jerry's good ideas, that's for sure," agreed Boris.

"Too right. We always seem to end up in trouble. Remember the time we went to Ireland, and he swore we could pretend to be Leprechauns?"

"And no one told us Leprechauns are only four feet high, so even the Irish knew we were telling tall stories. What with us all being over six foot," Fred recalled.

"And that trip to Italy? When he swore that tower thing was about to topple over, and had us straighten it up a bit?"

"You mean a lot."

"Whatever. Himself got us out of gaol that time, but it should have been a warning."

Mungo groaned, as Dai shifted his weight.

"Sorry," called Dai insincerely.

"What did he get last year then?" asked Mungo.

Fred looked at Dai, then back at Mungo. "He's the bass player. Probably forgot and put his stocking out after the New Year."

"Oh come on, even bass players get *something*."

"Lessons?"

"Strings?"

"Sympathy?"

The tour bus swung round some hairpin bends, and Mungo was silenced for a while. Then the Sprinter slowed, and turned onto a bumpy track. Mungo became quite vocal then.

"Why am I here?" he groaned, to general indifference.

"Where are we?" he asked. This too was ignored, not least because Dai, GG, Felldyke and Scar had all dozed off, and the other Little Helpers were not in a position to see out of the windows. The minibus bumped to a stop.

"We're here!" called Jerry in a relieved voice.

"Good!" exclaimed Mungo, feeling relieved that they had stopped before a slumbering dragon found relief of a different kind.

Fungus yawned, and climbed out of the tour bus, followed by Haemar.

"Looks different in the daylight," Fungus said.

"Yeah," agreed Haemar, less enthusiastically. Jerry climbed out of the Sprinter, and opened the side door. He jumped back smartly, as Felldyke fell sideways out of the Sprinter, and landed on the floor without waking up. Scar climbed stiffly down, using his drummer as a step, to be followed by GG and Dai.

Jerry stuck his head inside the van in search of his friends and colleagues. Well, colleagues, then. They groaned, and slid and crawled out onto the ground, by way of Felldyke who finally woke up.

"Are we there yet?" he asked, before opening his eyes and looking around. Then he woke up very fast indeed. "Here! Isn't this that vampire mechanic's place?"

Haemar walked round the front of the minibus and sighed. "Yes, but it's daylight, Felldyke."

"Oh, right." Felldyke looked bemused.

"Daylight? When vampires are asleep?"

"Oh, right!" Felldyke looked around the courtyard. Ahead lay a long, low, industrial building with various shutter doors, which were shuttered. Clearly a workshop. To his left was an attractive manor house, whose doors and windows were similarly guarded. To his right lay a selection of outbuildings which were clearly used for storage. Walking with some difficulty after the journey, Jerry approached the workshop.

"How's he going ter open up?" asked Haemar.

"That's easy," replied Fred. "We often have to turn up in the summer for the servicing and repair work, when the nights are short, so Idiot has given Jerry the code to operate the doors from the outside by remote."

"Why do yer call him Idiot?" asked Fungus.

"Well, would you give those codes to Jerry?" answered Fred.

Haemar and Fungus looked at each other, and nodded. That made sense.

"Isn't he worried that you might take off without paying?" asked Haemar.

Fungus nodded, for the same thought had occurred to him.

"Would you do that to a vampire? Seriously? And, the Sleigh belongs to Himself. You don't want to be in His bad books, I can tell you," warned Fred.

Jerry was pressing buttons on an entry system, whilst muttering to himself.

"See?" grumbled Fred. "Forget anything, Jerry can."

"Aha!" cried the maligned one, and with a rumble the roller shutter doors rolled upwards, revealing the large and empty workshop inside.

"Right!" said Fred, faintly surprised. "Let's get The Sleigh under cover."

Haemar waved at Eddie, who started the Sprinter, and carefully backed the trailer carrying The Sleigh into the workshop. Jerry stood at the back of the workshop, waving his arms to guide Eddie as he reversed back into the unlit workshop. Then he started waving his arms more urgently as The Sleigh continued into the workshop. At the last moment, Jerry dived under a workbench out of the way. The Sleigh juddered to a halt six inches from his nose.

"Der," called Eddie through his window.

"That's fine," called back Fred, peering into the workshop. "Right, Lads, all we need to do now is get it off the trailer."

"Typical," muttered Boris. "There's some work to be done, and Jerry vanishes."

"I'm here!" coughed Jerry, through a cloud of dust.

"He did go into the workshop," said Mungo.

"I'm under here!" yelled Jerry, hoarsely.

"Well, I can't see him," said Fred.

"Hello!"

Scar wandered down the side of the trailer, idly pulling at the straps of the coverings.

"Hey," he called back, "I think that there's someone under here."

"Too right there is!" complained Jerry, his voice reduced to a whisper.

"Is it Jerry?" called Mungo.

"Probably. Here, are you Jerry?"

"Yes!" wheezed Jerry, and sneezed.

"He thinks so," called Scar.

"Pity," mumbled Boris, under his breath.

"What are yer doing under there?" asked Scar.

"Keeping out of the way," replied Jerry. "Ugh, can you help me out? I don't think that anyone has ever cleaned under here in ages."

Scar bent down, grabbed the nearest bit of Jerry he could reach, and pulled, hard. Scar grunted with the effort, and Jerry yelled a bit louder. Dai joined them, and taking hold of Scar's belt, pulled as hard as he could. Jerry yelled again.

"He seems to be a bit stuck," complained Scar. Felldyke walked up, and he too reached under the workbench and seized whatever came to hand. The three hauled as hard as they could, and with a final asthmatic yell, and to the accompaniment of a long tearing sound, Jerry emerged in a cloud of dust, and as the two dwarfs fell over backwards, he landed on top of them. Dai started sniggering, and puffs of smoke and flame shot across the workshop, conveniently incinerating the "Victim of The Month" calendar hanging on the nearby wall.

The dust-cloud rose to the ceiling, and then dispersed. Jerry rose to his feet, and his trousers also dispersed. Scar averted his gaze.

"Some things aren't meant ter be seen by mortals," he complained.

"What have you done to my trousers?" wheezed Jerry, in disbelief. He gathered the shreds around himself, and tried to look dignified, as well as dishevelled.

"You can't go round looking like that!" warned Mungo.

"Tell me something I can't work out myself."

"Well, what are you going to do?" asked Boris.

Jerry glared at the Banned Underground, who had all gathered by

162

the trailer to laugh at his predicament.

"Stop laughing, or I'm make sure than none of you ever look forward to Christmas again!"

Fungus turned away to try and disguise his laughter. Haemar hid his face inside his helmet, and Scar hid behind Felldyke. GG, with a mighty effort, kept a po-faced expression.

"Der."

"What did he say?" asked Fred.

"Der," replied Fungus, helpfully.

"Yes, I heard that bit."

Haemar, with an effort, stifled his laughing fit. "Eddie said that we've got some spare gear in the boot of the tour bus. He can borrow some trousers."

With a haughty look, Jerry gathered the remains of his dignity, and strode to the Sprinter. The others left him to it, and started getting The Sleigh off Grizelda's trailer.

"Won't yer need the trailer?" asked Scar.

"No, once it's fixed, we'll get the reindeer and fly it back."

"So," worried Scar, "that means *we* have ter take the trailer back to Grizelda?"

"Could be worse," replied GG, quietly. "We could be waiting here for the mechanic to arise."

"The Vampire one?"

"Yes, Scar. Grizelda's a safer bet."

"I'd never normally use the word safer about her, but I know what yer mean."

At the back of the workshop, a chorus of grunts, shouts and complaints mainly from Dai, announced the removal of The Sleigh from the trailer. The trailer bounced as the load was removed, and the tow bar rose smartly to smack Jerry in the face as he rummaged in the clothes bag for something he was prepared to wear.

Scar and GG looked at each other.

"Are Santa's Little Helpers allowed to swear like that?" asked Scar.

"Well, not on duty, I'm sure," replied GG.

"Are you kidding?" asked Fred as he straightened up from examining one of the damaged runners on The Sleigh. "We spend ages having to take customer surveys from parents, watch TV adverts to monitor trends and, what was it? 'Maintain focus on responding to end-user demand in a volatile and fast moving consumer environment.'"

Scar looked perplexed. "What does that mean?"

"Damn kids can't make their minds up what they want. Is it any wonder we swear all the time back in the grotto? I mean, the language is so bad sometimes you'd think you were working with a bunch of football supporters, or hospital nurses."

"Nurses? Are they bad then?"

"Honestly," said Fred, "I went into hospital for a week last year, and when I came out I had a whole new vocabulary!"

Felldyke nodded gloomily. "I had the same experience. I had to look a number of words up when I came out, and I'm still not quite sure what a low carbohydrate diet is."

"Maybe, but I bet you're well acquainted with saturated fats," said Haemar. "Now come on, let's leave these lads to their business."

"Er, leave us? Where?" asked Mungo.

"Look," said Haemar, "we've brought yer all the way here. Now we need to get on."

"Where?" asked Felldyke.

Haemar sighed. "We need to record some more stuff for Adam, the record company, remember?"

"Oh, him."

"Fungus is going ter get us another gig, where we can put the recording gear out easily, isn't he?" agreed GG.

Dai looked enthusiastic.

Fungus turned a slightly deeper shade of green. "Well, now that you mention it," he started.

"Good!" interrupted Haemar. "That's settled. We'll leave yer to wait fer yer Vampire, then."

"DER!"

There was a brief dust cloud as The Banned jumped on board the minibus, galvanised by the reminder of the vampire mechanic. The Sprinter drove slowly out of the workshop and across the yard, the trailer bumping slightly as it ran over Mungo's foot.

"Did I see something move over there?" asked Scar, looking out of the side window.

"Der!"

The Sprinter accelerated, and sprinted across the courtyard and round the side of the house, leaving behind it a trail of dust and four disgruntled Little Helpers.

"Now what?" asked Boris.

"Why are you asking me?" asked Jerry.

"I've got to ask someone."

"Well, why not make a decision yourself?"

"I did. I decided to ask you."

Jerry sighed. "Look, we've managed to get The Sleigh here. All we have to do is wait for Idiot to wake up, and then get him to fix it, and we're on the way home. Sorted."

"It all sounds a bit too easy for me," grumbled Boris.

"Well, I don't see that we have any other choices," said Jerry. The others looked at each other, and then nodded glumly. They couldn't see any other choices either. Mungo yawned, and that set the others off, too.

"Stop yawning," he insisted, to no avail.

"Right," said Fred. "I'm going to have a kip."

"Where?" asked Mungo, looking around the workshop, which was well provided with ramps, toolboxes, and even an inspection pit in case any customers brought in a pit for inspection, but sorely lacking in anywhere to sleep.

"In The Sleigh, of course." Fred walked over to The Sleigh, and pulled the covers away. He promptly jumped in, and settled down in one corner. Boris looked at him.

"You know, we might as well follow his example. It's early

afternoon, we missed out on a night's sleep, and we've got to wait around for Idiot to wake up." He promptly jumped in beside Fred, and pulled a corner of the discarded coverings over himself.

Mungo and Jerry looked at each other, then shrugged and joined them. Jerry pulled the covers over the whole Sleigh,

and soon the only sounds to be heard in the workshop were the muffled snores.

Slowly, as they slept on, the shadows grew and lengthened, and the setting sun flared wildly against the horizon, painting vivid colours against the gathering gloom and shade of night. A little later, headlights picked out the entry to the courtyard, and with a muffled sound, a vehicle crunched across the gravel. The moonlight gleamed softly on the dark shape that emerged, and glided across the courtyard and through the open door of the workshop, it's whole posture an indication of danger and a terror of the night. A hand reached out gently, then with a violent motion pulled back and discarded the entire coverings from The Sleigh. The Little Helpers awoke on the spot, and with one voice, screamed at the figure towering above them.

Chapter Twelve

"Der?" asked Eddie.

"Back the way we came," Haemar told him.

"Where are we going then?" Dai wanted to know.

"Well, we borrowed this trailer from Grizelda, so we are going to take it back to her."

Dai nodded. He understood the need not to upset Grizelda, having met her a couple of times. "Has she mellowed at all?" he asked.

"No. Like a whisky, she seems to have got a bit more fiery as time goes on," muttered GG.

Dai nodded again. He wasn't quite following events yet, but wasn't worried. Someone else would be, so he just had to stay cool, have a few drinks, and play the bass. In that order, really.

In the front, Haemar and Fungus were arguing in low voices.

"Look, Fungus, I thought that you'd arranged a second gig round here!" insisted Haemar. "We did the Edern's benefit because you said we wouldn't have to travel far for the next one."

"Well," said Fungus defensively, "we won't. They'll have another gig in a few months. That'll be in the same place."

Haemar sighed. "Look, Fungus, we've had this arrangement for years. You find the gigs, I sort out the promoters, we all play the gig."

"Yeah."

"So, why haven't yer sorted out a gig then? The lads will be expecting one." Haemar glanced around and dropped his voice. He carried on without waiting to pick it up: "And Adam will be wanting some recordings before long. We've still got some of his cash left, but it's going down."

Fungus glanced around sideways, but the others were paying them no attention. Used to being left in the dark, the four other band members were occupying their journey time in their habitual fashion. GG was practising riffs on his Telecaster, Felldyke was eating, Scar was looking out of the window, and Dai was dozing.

"We made plenty from the benefit gig!" hissed Fungus.

"Yes, but after we've paid Eddie, paid the fuel card for the van, put a bit on one side for emergencies and covered the last few trips to the off license and the Fish n Chip shop, there's a big dent in it."

"Haemar, are you saying that we're broke?"

"No, Fungus. But I am saying that we need ter keep playing gigs. Look, the Bankers' Benefit paid well. But we lost money on that one we did in Leeds."

"How did we lose money?"

"Well, I made sure that the promoter covered the venue and our bar bill, but we still had ter pay for that hotel. And with the bill for the damage that Felldyke did in the bathroom when we tried ter make him get under that shower, well we might as well just have bought the hotel itself."

"Der."

"Yes, Eddie, I know I promised yer a bonus for cleaning up afterwards."

"Der."

"Yes, Eddie, we will pay it. Just, after the next gig if yer don't mind."

"Der."

"There's no need ter be like that. We're all in this together."

"Der."

"Yes Eddie, I know that there are other bands yer could work for. But we must be the most exciting!"

"Der. Der."

"Well, if you feel like that, I'll tell Grizelda all about it when we drop the trailer off."

"DER!"

"I knew that yer didn't really mean it."

"Der."

"We'll say no more about it. See, Fungus, that's called man management."

Fungus looked back at the assortment of dwarfs and a snoring dragon. "Bet it wouldn't work on them, then."

"It probably won't work on Adam, or those ants that follow him about, unless we can record some more stuff. Fungus, we need at least two more gigs by the end of the month!"

"Two, Haemar? Where am I going to find two decent gigs from? I mean, your not talking about just playing down the pub here, are you? We need a proper venue, for a start, just to get a sound balance."

"It's been ages since I fell over on stage!" called Scar from the back. He wasn't really listening in, but just reacted every time he heard those words. Haemar turned to glare at him.

"Shut up and go to sleep. Fungus and I are plotting."

"What, in the tourbus? Eddie will kill yer unless you clean up afterwards."

Haemar turned back to Fungus. "Look, Fungus, these mates of yours. Were they serious about organising this gig that they promised?"

"Well, yeah. But look, Haemar, it's not as if they are the most reliable, is it? I know what I found in me stocking last year, and it weren't what I'd asked for."

"OK, so what are we going ter do about getting another gig? And in a room big enough for us ter play, and with decent sound, so that we can record?"

"Der?"

"Yes, Eddie, turn left here."

"Der?"

"Yes, Eddie, besides the large village hall there."

"Der?"

"Yes, I said… beside… the…village…hall."

"Der."

"No, Eddie, there's no such skill as dwarf management."

"Der."

"Well, there's no need to snigger like that, either."

"Der."

"Yes, it is a good idea if you pull into the car park like that, and we'll find out how ter hire it."

"Haemar, how are we going to fill it?"

"Fungus, we're *The Banned Underground*. They'll all have heard of us."

"Who did you say you are?" asked the caretaker of the village hall.

"The Banned Underground," sighed Fungus.

"Well, this is the Miner's Institute. If you boys have been banned from the underground, I'm not sure we can let you book the hall, see. Like trade solidarity."

"No, we're a group. It's just a name."

"Well, I've never heard of you," grumbled the octogenarian caretaker.

"We're very well known in the North."

"Maybe, but this is Wales, and we're very particular you know. Can't have you playing here just because you want to come to a posh venue."

172

Fungus looked at the decaying village hall.

"And, you sound English to me," accused the caretaker.

Haemar looked perplexed. "I'm a dwarf. We come from all over."

"Ar, but are you an English Dwarf or a Welsh Dwarf?"

"I'm a Not Very Deep Dwarf. We live all over the place."

"And what is it that you play?"

"We're all bluesmen."

"It's a bit cold today, that's true," agreed the caretaker, "although your mate here looks a bit green."

"I'm quite a bit red," called Dai getting out of the minibus and stretching his wings in relief.

"Now then, that's a bit better! Here, you in the mock dragon skin, are you Welsh?"

"Course!" replied Dai indignantly.

"Prove it!"

"I cried for two days after we beat England to win the Six Nations Rugby tournament!"

"Proof positive!" agreed the caretaker, smiling. "Mind you, I didn't cry. I was too drunk. There will be no bother with the hall now, boys. When do you want it?"

"Er, tomorrow?"

"Then we'll give it a bit of a sweep out, look."

Back inside the minibus, Scar was watching the proceedings with some concern. "GG, I 'm worried."

"No change there then, Scar."

"No, I mean that I'm worried about Fungus."

"See a doctor, then. Or have a bath twice a year instead of once."

"I meant Fungus, not fungus. Everyone has fungus."

"Do they?"

"Felldyke always has."

"Yeah, but that's because he stores chicken drumsticks in his underpants."

"Whatever. Anyway, I'm worried."

"Scar, you're always worried. If they hold Olympics in it, you will be a cert for the British Team."

"Will they? It won't interfere with the tour dates will it?"

"Scar, it's years away. And I don't think that worrying is an Olympic Sport yet."

"Oh. Anyway."

"What?"

"I'm worried about Fungus. That Fungus. He's not himself."

"Who is he then?"

"Dunno, But, he's not bouncing about getting gigs, as he would normally."

"Well, yeah, I've noticed that."

"Maybe he's worried about something."

"That was last year, when Lakin, King Under the Mountain, had us by the short and curlies."

"Fungus hasn't got a beard, GG."

"It's just an expression, Scar. Just an expression."

"Like a frown?"

"Not really, well, all right, if you want."

"Well, I think he's worried, GG. Do yer think that it might be about this contract? The record deal?"

"We weren't paid enough fer it to be a record."

"But we've got to produce one, haven't we. And how are we ter do that, if we aren't gigging?"

GG sighed, and pointed out of the window at Fungus, Haemar and Dai who were all talking to the caretaker.

"Scar, there's yer answer. They are setting us up a gig."

"I agree with you Scar," muttered Felldyke without opening his eyes. "There's something odd about him at the moment."

"Aren't yer worried?"

"Scar, you worry enough fer all of us. Look, if Fungus can't cope, we'll just let Haemar take over. He's been itching ter do that for years."

"He's right, Scar," said GG putting his guitar away in its case. "Haemar's always wanted ter be the boss, what with being the singer. Most singers are, yer know."

"Power mad maniacs," muttered Scar.

"If they weren't they wouldn't be able ter sing. Sort of goes with the territory."

"Should we talk to him?"

"Why?"

"Well, we're all mates, if something is worrying him, should we ask if we can help?"

"Yer what? Help?"

"Well, if he's depressed or something, maybe it would do him good ter talk about it."

"Scar, if it's something that's bad enough ter worry Fungus, then I don't want to know about it. It would only worry me, and then there'd be more than one of us worried."

"Three," added Felldyke.

"Three?" asked GG.

"Well, if Fungus is worried, and then there's Scar, who is *always* worried, so if you were worried too, that'd be three."

"What about you, Felldyke?"

"I've got you lot ter do the worrying for me." Felldyke leant back in his seat and closed his eye again. Scar shook his head.

"Drummers."

"So," said Haemar to the caretaker, "that's sorted."

"Tidy," agreed Dai, in his best welsh accent.

"Not really," objected Fungus, looking through the doors into the village hall.

"Nothing wrong with the hall, boy," the caretaker sulked.

Haemar looked through the door too, and his jaw dropped. "Tell you what," he said, "we'll halve the fee unless you give it a clean."

The caretaker frowned. "Put ten quid in me pocket, and I'll make sure it's sorted for you then."

Haemar sighed, and fished in his pocket for some money. The caretaker's eyes gleamed, and both he and the money vanished back into the hall. Haemar slapped Fungus on the back, and all three turned to walk back towards the minibus.

"Now," said Haemar, "let's organise getting the word out."

"How are we going to do that?" asked Dai. Haemar grinned.

"We'll get Grizelda going on that!"

"Ah, yes," agreed the dragon. "That'll do the trick. And I've a few contacts round here."

"You, Dai?" asked Haemar, astonished. "What sort of contacts have you got round here?"

"Sheep farmers, mostly," confessed the dragon, with an appropriate look.

"Der!" called Eddie from the minibus as he started the engine. As the minibus pulled out of the car park, Haemar looked closely at Fungus and then riffled through the collection of CDs, before selecting some Etta James. He was relieved to see a smile cross his friend's face. Fungus delved into a pocket, extracted some Kendal Mint Cake that had seen better days, and popped some into his mouth. His eyes closed, he leant back in the seat. Etta James'

177

soulful voice echoed around the inside of the tour bus.

"Pity Haemar don't sing like that," muttered Felldyke. Scar reached across without looking, and shoved another drumstick deep into Felldyke's mouth. The drummer accepted the reproof, and the bus drove on.

All The Banned had relaxed nicely by the time Eddie pulled up beside Grizelda's caravan. But their arrival was enough to spoil that move.

"Are yer sure that we can't just leave the trailer and go?" asked GG, disconnecting the tow hitch from the Sprinter.

"Look," Haemar said, as he pushed the trailer towards the back of the caravan, "We don't really know anyone around here. But you can bet that *she* does by now."

"Yes, but most of them are probably sat in ponds," replied GG.

"I heard that, Gormless!"

GG went white under his beard, and slowly straightened up from the trailer.

"I don't turn everyone into frogs yer know," grumbled Grizelda, and closed the window of the caravan. There was a sigh of relief, cut short when the door was opened and Grizelda appeared in person.

"Oh, er, well," GG stammered.

"Oh shut up. Thank you for bringing the trailer back. Me husband, Ben, will be wanting it back in a day or so."

"Er, no, thanks for the loan," said Haemar.

"Where's that Fungus, then?" asked Grizelda. Haemar walked up to her and, showing an unaccustomed bravery, took her arm and

178

pulled her round the side of the caravan.

"I'm worried about him," he hissed into Grizelda's ear. She frowned.

"What do yer mean?"

"Well, he keeps going quiet, won't talk much, don't smile. Yer know Fungus, he's always having a good time, even when he isn't, if yer follow me. I think he's depressed."

"Fungus? What could make him depressed? He used to live in my cellar."

"I don't know, really."

"Well, you know how he's normally full of energy? He's not. Seems run down. Listless."

"How long have you lot been touring now?"

"Dunno. Long time."

Grizelda smiled. Haemar flinched. Grizelda misinterpreted this as concern for Fungus, instead of fear, and smiled again. "I can fix him, overnight."

"You can?"

"Easy. Wish I could fix these blasted Vampires so easy. Send him over here. Fungus is a friend of mine, can't have him unwell."

"Is it serious?"

"Only if I don't fix him." Grizelda fixed Haemar with a sharp stare. "Go get him now."

Haemar backed away around the corner of the caravan, and a

moment or two later reappeared with a less than enthusiastic Fungus. Grizelda took his arm, and glared at Haemar until he retreated. A few minutes later, Grizelda walked into view. Fungus had vanished. The Banned looked at each other. No one wanted to be the first to ask.

"So," said Grizelda, "What else are you wanting off me? Or can I go ter work now? It's startin' to get dark."

"Well," started Haemar, "we've got this gig."

"Oooh, good!" said a voice in his ear. Haemar jumped. The Count winced as a heavily armoured dwarf landed on his foot, but centuries of good breeding helped him to keep quiet and not complain.

"We loved your last show," agreed Hugo, appearing beside Felldyke.

Scar and GG took a step backwards, but stopped as Percival put an arm around each of them, from behind.

"You had me dancing!" Percival agreed.

Scar smiled, gingerly. When nothing bad, or exciting happened, GG copied him.

"Now, now, " said Grizelda to the vampires. "You know what I've told you about small snacks between meals. Go away and get yerselves fed properly. I've got some jobs for you to do. Tonight, we are doing occupational therapy!"

"None of the occupations I ever had were therapeutic," complained Hugo.

Percival looked at him. "What occupations were they, then?"

Hugo delved into his memory. "Let's see, now: I've herded goats, chopped wood, and loaded bales of straw,"

"What did yer do?" asked GG.

"I was a man at arms."

"Oh." GG was obviously unenlightened.

"Basically, it's a cross between a squire and a squaddie," explained Hugo. "I had to clean my master's kit, get his meals and keep him out of trouble."

"And now yer a Vampire!"

"Yes," sighed Hugo. "And now I have to clean his kit, get his meals and keep him out of trouble."

"So, what's changed?"

"I get a better class of trouble to avoid."

"And this lot are trouble you are going or avoid!" insisted Grizelda. "Go away. Come back in an hour. This lot are playing tomorrow, and you three are flyin' around, putting up some posters."

Scar turned to GG. "I always wondered why they were called fly posters."

"I always though that they meant posters about flies, myself."

The Count nodded. "There's a printer in town that's open late. We'll call in there for a drink, and bring some posters back with us. Have you any ideas about them?"

Haemar reached into a pocket, and pulled out a rather creased flyer from the last gig but one. "This will do, just change the date," he said.

"Right!" The Count beckoned to his followers, and they duly followed him off into the dark sky. When they had faded to grey, the Reindeer cautiously appeared around the side of the caravan. Grizelda looked at them fondly.

"Bless," she said. "They don't seem ter like The Count."

Haemar shivered slightly. "Can't think why."

"Look," said Grizelda, "that caravan there is empty. Why don't you lot go and have a kip? Eddie there looks a bit tired."

"What about Fungus?"

"He'll be right as rain by the morning. Go on. And I'm really grateful to you lads."

"Why?" asked Scar, suspiciously.

"Because I've now got a great excuse to get rid of that lot and have an evening off. And get paid fer it. Works for me."

Felldyke was trying, unsuccessfully to open the door of the nearby caravan. Grizelda smiled. She waved a hand at the door, which opened. Felldyke staggered backwards, and fell over.

"What will the park owner say to us stopping here?" worried Scar.

"Rivet, probably," Grizelda told him.

Scar swallowed, and wisely stayed silent.

"Well, thanks for the accommodation, then," said Haemar.

"Er, yeah, thanks, Gizelda," muttered the others.

"Der."

"Yeah, ta."

"Least I can do. I do get a ticket, don't I? To the gig?"

"Course! It's pay on the door, but Eddie will just let yer in."

"Der! Der!"

Grizelda nodded, satisfied.

The Banned trooped into the caravan, and found places to collapse.

"Haemar," Scar asked as sleep overwhelmed him. "Where's Fungus then?"

"Grizelda took him off. Probably best not to ask. But one thing I know, she'll take care of him"

"Sort of what I were worried about."

Chapter Thirteen.

(Or, maybe, Twelve sharp.)

(Fourteen flat, possibly.)

The Watches needed no second invitation to leave the hut. Ned staggered as the junior and the assistant assistant pushed past him, out into the night, Ned stared at the figure standing by the door.

"Why are you helpin' us to get away?" he asked suspiciously.

"I don't care for Druids. I had a SatNav myself once."

Ned nodded, and felt the sympathetic vibration in his pocket.

"Come on," said the Vampire Mechanic. "Let's get gone before these crazed sun worshippers wake up."

"Um, the hearse would appear to be in a field, if I remember correctly?"

"I took it out before breakfast."

"Right," said Ned, slowly. "So you have, erm, eaten already?"

"I'm not keen on Druids, but they'll do. Especially when they try to interfere."

"What do you intend to do with us?"

"You said that you wanted to talk to me? That your boss had sent you? I thought that I'd at least listen."

"Good." Ned felt relieved, and the need to relieve himself receded.

"Get in the hearse. I'll drive."

The Dark Wizards climbed into the hearse, and the Vampire Mechanic drove off. Behind them, various druids in various stages of undress, collected by the roadside.

"Who was that masked man?" asked one.

"What makes you think he wore a mask?" asked a senior druid, rubbing the puncture marks on his throat.

"Well, his face was black and white, so I thought…"

"No, Trust me on this. It wasn't a mask."

"And, he had these big fake teeth like the ones I got from the joke shop."

"They weren't fake. Trust me on this, too."

The Chief Druid, his robes covered in mud, glared after the retreating hearse. "Must be Monday," he grumbled.

"Tell me, why?" asked his colleagues.

"Because I don't like Mondays."

The black hearse turned a corner, and was lost to their sight.

"How should we address you, sir?" asked the junior wizard.

"You can call me Basil. Everyone calls me Basil."

"Right, er, Basil, so where are we going?"

"Besides away from the spot where you were going to be sacrificed to the Sun God?"

"Good answer, good answer," muttered the assistant assistant.

"Back to my place. From there, you can make your way off to where ever it is you want to go."

"Thanks," said Ned, surprised.

"Now, what did your boss want to talk about? And, who is he?"

"Well, our boss, is The Grey Mage, from round Keswick way."

"I've heard about him. He's supposed to be a pretty good accountant. I'd been thinking of talking to him." The Vampire Mechanic smiled, toothily. "Another reason not to add you three to my stock, then."

The junior swallowed, hard. "Stock?" he managed to ask.

"Well, besides being a mechanic, I am a vampire. Got to make a living you know."

"Or an Un-living" muttered the assistant assistant. Basil ignored him.

"Carry on," Basil instructed Ned.

"Well, he'd heard that you have some dealings with Himself, or Himself's staff?"

"I deal with a lot of people."

"But not too many use a vintage Sleigh stuffed full of complicated electronics."

Basil was quiet, and looked at Ned for so long that he missed a turn in the road, and nearly collided with an oncoming lorry. When alerted (by the screaming from the back seat) Basil skilfully avoided a collision by forcing the lorry off the road. The assistant assistant relieved his feelings by opening the window, and setting fire to the back wheels of the lorry with a well aimed spell. Ned overlooked this insubordination, and tried to still his wildly beating heart.

"The Sleigh," mused Basil.

Ned nodded.

"I used to do them both, you know."

"Both?" asked Ned. "I thought there was just one."

"Oh no, there's two. Santa has one, and Notsanta has another."

"Not Santa?" asked the assistant assistant, confused.

"Notsanta. Think Evil Twin syndrome, and you've got the idea. You wouldn't want him turning up to fill your stocking, instead of Himself, I can assure you."

"I've never heard of Notsanta," said Ned.

"Well, he's only been around for fifty years or so. Of course, once He was here, He fitted in so well that it was like He'd always been here."

"Where did He come from?" asked the junior.

"The story I heard is that he was a Traffic Warden, who tried to put a ticket on The Sleigh, and got cursed."

"But they get cursed every working day. Aren't they immune?"

"When Santa curses you, you know about it. It's a bit different to a motorist making scandalous claims about your mother. Anyway, Himself had a spare Sleigh, so Notsanta got that one."

Ned nodded. Again.

"I've been maintaining them both now since the last war. And it's no joke. Getting the parts is a nightmare. Then, getting paid for the work, well."

"Can't you refuse to let the vehicles out until you've been paid?" asked the assistant assistant, who as a professional taxi driver, had a lot of experience with garages.

Basil laughed, a little bitterly. "I did try that, once. Got a visit from some guy, claimed to be Himself's accountant. Accountant! Huh! I might be a vampire, but I don't want him round again."

"We're accountants," said the junior. Unnecessarily, in Ned's view. Ned had an excellent view of Basil's expression. And his teeth. Particularly his teeth.

"After that, we reached a compromise. I do The Sleigh, and some dwarfs in the town do The Notsleigh. Both come in for necessary repairs, and once a year they get a service. The Notsleigh is in with the dwarfs at the moment, and The Sleigh is due with me in a couple of weeks."

"Our boss has this computer program, and it said that The Sleigh were on the move, so he guessed it were coming down here," continued Ned.

"And?"

"And The Grey Mage wanted us to liberate it."

"He wanted you to steal Santa's Sleigh? Whatever for?" Basil was astonished. "In a long life, and longer after-life, I have rarely heard anything so nutty."

"Well, his mercedes estate isn't very well," Ned explained.

"In what way?"

"A dragon landed on its roof."

"That will do it every time," agreed Basil.

"He thought that we might be able ter persuade you to let us run off with it."

"Persuade me?"

"Well, bribe you."

"I'll have you know that I'm a member of a lot of Trade Associations. They are all against that sort of thing."

"Oh."

"How much did he offer?"

Ned leant across and whispered a sum.

"Three times that, and I'll look the other way."

"Three times! He could buy a new Mercedes with that!"

"But it wouldn't be dragon-proof, would it?"

Ned nodded. Basil had made a good point. "What could yer do for what I originally offered? That's all the budget, really."

The vampire mechanic thought deeply, as he guided the van onto the driveway to his house and workshop. He pulled up.

"Here's an offer, then."

All three Dark Wizards leant closer, eagerly anticipating a way of achieving their ends.

"Give me a load of cash, and I'll get you into the workshop where they keep the Notsleigh. After all, if your boss is a Dark Lord, then the Notsleigh might be a better bet for him, don't you think?"

Ned nodded.

"Will you stop that," muttered the assistant assistant, fed up of the nodding.

"Don't blame me," replied Ned. He turned back to the driver. "You've got a deal."

"One other thing."

"Go on," sighed Ned.

"You three get yourselves ready for a fight."

The junior wizard and the assistant assistant grabbed the door handles, ready to break out and run.

"Not with me," Basil said reassuringly. "But there's some lights round the back of the workshop, where there shouldn't be. Intruders. I might need a hand."

"No worries," said Ned, and shook his arms in his sleeves. The Vampire Mechanic waved his arm, and all the doors flew open. Leaving the van, he and The Watches slowly walked down the drive. Reaching the corner of the house, Basil motioned with his arm, and they all leapt around into the courtyard.

"Aaaarrgghh," yelled the assistant assistant as his energetic leap landed him on a rather slippery drain cover, and he slid towards the dark shapes of the intruders on his back.

Ned and the junior both yelled out loud as they fell over the sliding body of their comrade. The intruders all yelled loudly too, but fortunately for them Basil recognised the yells of terror just as he was about to strike.

"Jerry? Mungo? What are you doing here?" he asked.

"Is that you?" asked Jerry, unable to take his eyes from a sharp set of teeth positioned almost two millimetres from his throat.

"If it wasn't, why would I be asking your name?"

"Because it's not polite to eat strangers?"

Basil released his grip, and Jerry sank to the floor, shaking.

"What are you doing here?" asked Basil.

"Er, well, we had a bit of a problem," said Boris, before a yelling group of Dark Wizards charged into him and added to his problems by knocking him under the workbench.

"Is this The Sleigh?" asked the junior wizard, from underneath it.

"Er, yes," agreed Mungo.

Ned climbed to his feet, and brushed a lot of dust off his clothing. He walked around The Sleigh, examining it with astonishment. "Your Boss is a worse driver than our boss," he observed.

"Ah," said Mungo.

Basil was walking around The Sleigh with a critical eye. "In my professional opinion," he started.

"Yes?" asked Mungo eagerly.

"It's knackered. Goosed. Killed, stone dead, trashed. Tell Himself to scrap it, and buy a new one."

191

"Ah," said Mungo.

Basil gave him a very hard look. "Is there something you want to tell me, then?"

"It was all Jerry's fault!"

"Oh no it wasn't!" exclaimed Jerry, emerging from the space under the workbench.

"Oh yes, it was," chorused his friends.

"Oh no it wasn't!" insisted Jerry.

"Oh, yes it was," replied the assistant assistant. Everyone turned to look at him.

"Sorry, force of habit," he muttered.

"Look, you were driving when we hit that hill," Boris insisted. "Not me, not Fred, not Mungo."

"Yes, but that was just a coincidence."

Boris turned to The Vampire Mechanic who had been observing all this with a weary expression.

"Look, sir, I'm going to tell you the truth."

Basil looked shocked. "That's going to be a first for my customers."

"What do yer mean?" asked the junior wizard.

"Well, normally they try telling me that a tree jumped out into the road, or that a cow made a forced landing in their path, or that the council moved a wall when they weren't looking."

"Hahahahah," laughed the taxi driving assistant assistant. "I used the one about the wall last year! No one believed me then, either!"

Santa's Little Helpers maintained a dignified silence.

"Oh come on, I'm a professional driver. Those are just so funny.
Only a complete idiot…would say…any one of those…"

"Well, they did move that wall," muttered Jerry.

"And I'd swear that tree moved," grumbled Mungo.

"The cow ran out of gas," said Fred, sulkily.

"This time it was the Reindeer," said Boris.

"They never run out of gas. It's all the greens they eat," Basil
commented. "So, what did you really do?"

"We hit a hill."

"Did it jump out at you?" asked the assistant assistant.

Boris glared at him. "No."

"A hill." Basil walked all around The Sleigh in complete silence,
pausing every now and then to suck his teeth in admiration.

"Was this an Official Trip?" he asked from underneath the heavily
damaged front.

"Er."

"Of course," said Jerry, brightly. "We thought that we would
deliver The Sleigh to you a couple of weeks early, in the hope that
you could have it ready by the time Himself comes back from his
holiday."

"Santa takes a holiday?" asked the junior wizard.

Mungo looked faintly surprised. "Yes. He usually goes on a cruise round the Bahamas."

"The Bahamas?"

"Yes. Somewhere warm and he doesn't have to drive."

"Doesn't he get recognised?"

"What, without the red suit? Not often. Of course it does happen."

"And what then?" asked Ned, fascinated.

"There's another mysterious disappearance in the Bermuda triangle. That's what's happened to all those ships down the years. Nothing to do with the aliens. They've learnt to steer well clear of Himself."

"And they are too busy surfing, anyway," agreed Jerry.

"And the aircraft?" asked the assistant assistant.

"Spotted him on his way to or from the cruise ship. I tell you, you really don't want to be on the wrong side of Himself."

"That Flight 19 went all over the show before they vanished," Ned objected.

"Yeah, well, they were military. They took better avoiding action before he could get a missile lock on them."

"So, what's Himself going to say when he sees the state of this?" asked Boris.

"Well, we were hoping that, erm," started Mungo.

"What, that I can fix *that*?" asked Basil.

"Well, now that you mention it," Mungo muttered.

194

Basil gave him a hard look, and an avaricious smile. Mungo sighed. He didn't need a phrase book to interpret the meaning behind the expression. Basil walked around The Sleigh again, shaking his head and sucking his teeth.

"You know that this is going to cost, don't you?"

"Is it?" asked Jerry, artlessly. "It is the normal service isn't it?"

"Normal service? *Normal service?* The secondary propulsion unit is covered in mud and sat on the back seat instead of being properly mounted. The runners are hanging off and the electronics have longed out."

"Longed out?"

"Same as shorted out, only more so."

"I've seen Himself bring it back like this before," insisted Jerry.

"When?"

"What about the time Himself got caught in that hurricane?"

"Water damage, that was. This is a bit more solid."

"OK, we're over a barrel here," admitted Jerry.

"Where?" asked Fred, looking around.

"It's just an expression," Boris told him.

"Well, I might be able to do something for you," said Basil slowly.

"Bet he wants blood," grumbled Fred.

"I hope that's just an expression too," Boris told him, looking at The Vampire Mechanic sucking his teeth again.

"Me too."

"Right," said Basil. "Here's my offer."

Jerry and Mungo looked anxious.

"I'll get it fixed for you."

Jerry and Mungo looked brighter.

"But it will cost you."

"How much?" sighed Jerry.

The Vampire Mechanic thought carefully. "Normal service costs, obviously. Plus I want you to authorise the extras I'll charge for sorting out the electrics. I'll say that they've corroded. And that I've found some bodywork that wants doing. And work on the guidance systems. You'll have to certify to Himself that all this work is kosher."

Jerry breathed a big sigh of relief, and Boris and Fred hugged each other.

"And," added Basil.

Mungo went very still.

"I shall want a favour."

"What favour?" asked Mungo.

"I don't know yet. When I think of one, I'll let you know." Basil showed all of his teeth.

"Er," said Mungo.

"Done!" agreed Jerry, quickly.

Ned nudged his junior in the ribs. "That's creative negotiation fer you. Watch and learn."

"So," continued Basil, "who's going to help me get The Sleigh onto the ramps? And this is not a rhetorical question."

The night was wearing out by the time that Santa's Little Helpers, helped by Ned and his assistants, finally had The Sleigh balanced safely on the repair ramp and ready for attention.

"That's sorted. Everybody out," instructed Basil. When everyone had gathered just outside the workshop, Basil closed the roller shutter doors, standing just inside the workshop. As the doors clattered to the floor, the Little Helpers and The Watches suddenly realised that they were stood in the courtyard, and The Vampire Mechanic had locked himself, The Sleigh, and crucially the only available transport inside his secure workshop.

"Here," complained Boris, "there's nowhere to sit!"

"Then go in the bushes, like everyone else," Jerry told him.

Boris looked around to see various heads already concealed amongst the foliage at the side of the courtyard. Cries of relief echoed around.

"Well, what are we going to do now? We can't sit here all day," grumbled Boris a few minutes later.

"Well, we're walking into the town," announced Ned.

He received some pointed looks from his juniors, but shot them a significant glance, and they shut up.

"I know!" said Fred. "There's decent pub not too far away, you remember it from last year?"

Jerry and Mungo nodded. The Watches pulled Ned to one side,

almost out of earshot.

"Walk?" asked the assistant assistant, in the aggrieved tones of a professional taxi driver.

"Walk?" asked the junior wizard, in the aggrieved tones of the terminally idle.

"Walk," said Ned firmly. He bent closer to the others as they leant towards him, and all three heads met with a bang.

"Walk," insisted Ned, blinking. "I have, in my hand, a piece of paper."

"Neville Chamberlain had one of those. It didn't do him much good," warned the junior, darkly.

"This one has the address of the workshop where the other Sleigh is. And its opening times," explained Ned. "By extension, it's closing times, if you follow me."

"Ah," said the junior.

"Right," said the assistant assistant.

"And is it near here?" asked the junior.

"Nearish," said Ned.

"Nearish?"

"We'll have ter get a lift. It's probably a bit far to walk."

The junior wizard gave the assistant assistant a hard look. "Anywhere but the pub is too far fer him to walk," he said to Ned.

"Well, the pub's a start. We can get a taxi from there."

"We usually get some rooms at the pub," Jerry said walking up to

The Watches. "Come on lads," he called over his shoulder. "We'll show you the way," he said to Ned.

Grumbling loudly, The Watches joined the Little Helpers and they all trudged off up the drive away from the workshop.

In the darkness of the workshop, the Vampire Mechanic listened to their footsteps leaving, and smiled. Picking up a quart of oil, he took a long drink, then walked over to The Sleigh, and sighed deeply. After checking that the workshop was completely secure against the unwanted intrusion of daylight, he walked back over to The Sleigh, and picked up a spanner.

Chapter Fourteen

Dabbing his mouth with a handkerchief, Count Notveryfarout walked out of the printers with a big roll of posters under his arm.

"Hugo? Percival?" he called, and sighed when he realised that his fellow vampires were not waiting outside for him.

"Hugo!" he yelled.

"No need to shout," came the reply and the two other vampires slid around the corner looking a bit sheepish.

"Where have you two been then?"

"The butcher had a late night opening."

"Ah."

"So, we're ready to go. What does she want us to do?"

"I've got these fly posters." The Count held up some sheets of paper.

"Special Tonit. One night only," read Hugo slowly. "Tonit?"

"Printers' error. She must have been distracted at the time," said the Count, licking his lips reflectively.

"So, what do we do now with the fly posters?"

"Get flying. I've got some paste here, so get around the town and put them up anywhere you think that people will see them. But don't be seen."

"Hang on," objected Hugo. "If we're not supposed to be seen, how do we put the posters where they will be seen?"

"Use some imagination!" retorted the Count, and walked off.

Percival and Hugo looked at each other, bemused.

"How about the coach station?" suggested Percival.

"Good idea! People have to hang about for ages there with nothing to do!"

"And the railway station?"

"Yes, there's always a queue forming there too."

"And the Police station?"

"Do people hang about there with nothing to do but look at posters?"

"Besides the police, you mean?"

"Right."

The two vampires walked off into the night…

"Look, sergeant, I'm sure that they didn't mean any harm," sighed Grizelda.

"Loitering is a serious offence, Madam."

"Loiterin'?"

"My officers observed them for a long time."

"Why?"

"Well, it's been a quiet night, and they didn't have anything better to do."

"No, sergeant, I meant why were your lads watching them?"

"They were seen behaving suspiciously with a pot of glue and these here." The sergeant unrolled the last remaining poster advertising a certain gig. "They were followed around the town, and observed posting a lot of these in inappropriate places."

"What's an inappropriate place for a fly poster?" asked Grizelda.

"The airport for a start. And the front windscreen of a train. They put several on the sides of coaches, quite a few bus stops, and then they started on the council offices."

"So? Public information, that is."

"Yes, but then they tried informing the Public at the Conveniences and even pasted one on our front door!"

"Yes, sergeant, I saw it on the way in. I were a bit surprised that you hadn't removed it."

"Oh, we can't take them down. They're classed as evidence now."

"What about the ones at the council offices?"

"That's worse. Health and Safety said that as the posters were six feet off the ground, the Council Highways lads would need scaffolding to get up to them to remove them. And, they can't put up scaffolding on the street without getting a footpath closure order from the Council. That will take at least a month to go through the committee stage."

"Where else did they go then?"

"All along the watchtower, down by the riverside, down by the Lake, for starters."

"Well, I'm sure that they are very sorry, sergeant. And if they aren't now, then they're going ter be, I assure you."

"Madam, I cannot just release them. They've been charged!"

"What with?"

"Batons and riot gear, mostly. They didn't want to come quietly."

"I see. Well, I think justice would be best served if you turned them over to me. And that's not the soft option."

"Madam! I couldn't possibly agree... Rivet, rivet,... I'll get the keys now. But we'll have to attend this concert, by, who are they? The Banned Underground? They'll have to answer some serious questioning. We can't allow this sort of thing to happen in a holiday town."

"What, you mean entertaining yer visitors?"

"It's taken a hundred years to get our reputation for being dull. Don't want to ruin it now. I'll just let them out."

The sergeant led Grizelda towards the cells, and opened a door.

"It's *her!* Can we go back in the cell, please?" said Percival, clasping Hugo by the arm.

"Why are you asking me?" asked Hugo, trying to stand behind his fellow.

"Come on, you two," said Grizelda firmly.

"Us?"

"Well, not him." She glared at the police sergeant, who hurriedly pushed past the two vampires into the cell, and pulled the door shut behind him.

Grizelda turned on her heel, and the other policeman dived over the desk and hid. Grizelda allowed herself a small smile of satisfaction, as she led the way out of the building. "So," she asked sternly, "who's going to be the first to tell me a convincing lie?"

"He is!" replied Hugo and Percival in unison, each pointing at the other.

Grizelda sighed. "So, how far did you get with the posters?"

"We've been everywhere!" asserted Hugo.

"River deep and mountain high," agreed Percival, who was feeling weary from the exertion.

"So how come you got yerselves arrested? Why didn't you either fly or drink your way out?"

"Well, Grizelda, you have been telling us not to draw attention to ourselves, and to be discreet. We thought that snacking on policemen might be classed as anti-disestablishmentarianism," Hugo told her.

"Really?" asked Grizelda, who didn't actually know what that was* but didn't want to admit to it.**

*[Like most of us.]

**[Like all of the rest of us. Including Hugo.]

"And Count Notveryfarout is very strong on law and order."

"Well, his laws and his orders, anyway," added Percival.

"And we knew that we were allowed one phone call, and who better than your good self to rescue us from durance vile?"

"Didn't look that vile ter me," muttered Grizelda.

Percival secretly agreed, as the cell had been substantially cleaner than the witch's caravan.

"And here we are. The posters are all up, so The Banned should get a decent audience, no harm done."

"Well, except to that railway worker."

What happened to him?" asked Grizelda, not entirely sure that she wanted the answer.

"Well," said Hugo, "he came along just when we were fixing posters onto an intercity train. So, we glued him to the front of it, and concealed him with dirt."

"Is that all?"

"No, we gave him a camcorder for the next journey. He'll probably be selling the footage on eBay next week, once they've edited his screams out."

"Ah. Right."

"So, can we go back to the caravan now, please? The night is becoming worn out."

"I know how it feels. Yeah, come on. No point in hanging around here, since you've run out of posters."

Behind them, further advertising was being planned.

"Right!" said the sergeant, making some changes to the poster he had shown Grizelda. "Take this to the printer, and get them to run us some off quickly!"

The Police Constable examined the text. "Wanted for questioning," he read slowly.

"And get them posted up all around the town before lunch!" the sergeant called after him.

Slowly, Dawn spread her rosy light across the caravan park, reflecting that at least some areas of the World were sufficiently attractive to provide her with some job satisfaction. Regrettably, this wasn't one of them.

Dai The Park, the owner of the caravan park, emerged from his imposing one bedroom bungalow, and after yawning widely looked around his demesne with a lordly glance. All was quiet. Those (un)fortunate enough to be occupying his caravans were still soundly asleep. So, with the care and consideration for the wellbeing and happiness of his customers that is so typical of holiday park owners, he dragged his petrol driven lawnmower from the shed and started maintaining the grass, paying particular attention to the areas around the occupied caravans.

Happily for Dai, the lawnmower made such a loud noise that he was unaware of the chorus of complaints and abuse that followed his progress around the park. The noise from the badly silenced two-stroke engine was sufficiently menacing to prevent The Reindeer objecting to his activities, and they withdrew to a quieter area.

Eventually, the racket aroused the members of the Banned, as they rested.

"Are you snorin' again?" demanded Haemar.

"Who, me?" asked GG.

"No, him!"

"I don't snore," mumbled Dai, before sinking back into sleep.

Another rumbling noise shook the caravan.

"It were you!" accused Haemar.

"Who, me?" asked GG.

"No, him!"

"Can't have been Dai, he's asleep."

"Oh, right," grumbled Haemar.

This time the rasping snarl took place just feet from Haemar's head, and he sat up with a jolt. And lay back down quickly, when his head and the underside of the table tried to occupy the same space/time co ordinates without the benefit of quantum.

"Ow!" The swearing rose in intensity, as did the bump on Haemar's head.

"Told you he were snoring!" complained Haemar.

GG opened one eye, but quickly closed it again, for his own safety. His ears were a better guide to events in the dim lit caravan, anyway. "That noise isn't Dai. It's in the wrong key. His snores are a bit lower than that."

Haemar settled down, and listened more carefully to the raucous noise. Then, careless of his personal safety, he crawled from under the table, climbed over Dai who was lying on the seat beside him, and flung the curtains open. Sunlight flooded into the caravan, and if it were possible, would have fled back out again quickly.

"Wassa matter? Something wrong?" asked Scar, rousing from sleep.

"It's too early in the day for anything ter have gone wrong yet," GG reassured him.

Slowly, now that Dai The Park had driven away laughing manically to seek fresh victims, The Banned emerged from their deep refreshing slumbers, and looked around the inside of the caravan.

"Yeuch," observed GG.

"It's worse than the dressing rooms we normally get," agreed Scar.

"Apart from the size, it looks quite homely to me," Dai disagreed.

"Where's Felldyke?" asked Haemar.

A brief search revealed the drummer, still slumbering, underneath a rather large pile of empty pizza boxes.

"Did we get through all that lot last night?" asked Scar.

"Must have done," GG agreed.

"Der."

"Well, we had a few drinks," rumbled Dai, "then Felldyke and Eddie had the munchies, and Haemar-"

"Why are yer bringing me into this?"

"Well, you were in charge of the kitty."

Haemar looked around for the large, solid bag. It was close to the table, but the top was open, and the contents few.

"We've been robbed!" he exclaimed.

"I thought that pizza delivery bloke wanted a lot of money."

"Der."

"And what about that bloke what delivered all the beers from the shop up the road?"

"Yer right there, Scar. I thought that he looked a bit dodgy too."

"But Haemar agreed to pay them, didn't he lads?" pointed out Felldyke.

Haemar looked stricken. "Tell me one thing, lads, before I have to admit to Fungus that we've just blown what was left of the take from the gig, *did we enjoy ourselves?* Because the thing is, I can't remember."

"Der."

"Must have done," muttered Scar, and then cheered up. "We must have done. It's always been a great party when you can't remember it the next day!"

"Yeah, right!" agreed GG.

"And, and, and we needed to relax, didn't we?" suggested Dai.

"Der!"

"You weren't at the gig," pointed out Haemar.

"But, I needed to relax anyway. Got to be ready for tonight!"

"What's tonight?" asked Felldyke.

"We're playing this local village hall," GG reminded him.

"Oh. Not the classy venues we've been getting used to then?"

"Unfortunately, not," Haemar agreed. "But, it will raise some cash, and give us a chance to record some more tracks. In fact, I think that when we've had some breakfast, we should go and rehearse."

"Haemar," objected Scar, "we're professionals! When have we ever rehearsed?"

"I reckon we should start. Anyone disagrees, and they can tell Fungus about last night."

"Talkin' of Fungus, where is he?" asked GG.

"Grizelda took him off with her," Scar reminded them.

"Der! Der!"

"Don't panic, Eddie, they're friends. She won't have frogged him. Will she? Haemar?"

"Na, they've been mates for years," muttered Haemar. "He used to live in her cellar for ages."

"You know, he's not been himself fer some time," said GG.

"Who has he been then?" asked Dai, curious.

"No, I mean he's just...not been...how he normally is."

"Too much of that Kendal Mint Cake, I reckon. All that sugar can't be good fer him."

"Why's that Scar?" asked GG.

"Well, he's a BogTroll, right? Mebbe the sugar's been fermenting inside him."

"What, like yeast? How's that infectious?"

210

"My aunt had a yeast infection," put in Felldyke.

"More like the other way round," muttered Scar, who had once met Felldyke's aunt.

"Der?"

"Eddie's right. What do you reckon that she's done with him?"

"I agree that he's been out of sorts recently. Probably Grizelda's taken him off for some of that spiritual healing."

"As long as she gets him back in time fer tonight," worried Scar.

"She will," asserted Haemar with a confidence that he didn't quite feel.

"Gotta have Fungus," agreed Felldyke.

"You've got me," snarled Haemar.

"Yes, yes, we know," soothed GG. "But you don't play the sax."

"I do all the vocals!"

"Come on lads," Dai quelled the incipient argument.

"Yeah, Haemar, of course we need you, don't we lads?" agreed GG quickly.

There came a rumbling of assent from all sides, and Haemar sat down again, mollified.

"Right then," said Scar quickly, "I vote that we go into town, find a decent cafe and have some breakfast, then go and rehearse." He looked aside, and then quickly added: "Just as Haemar suggested!"

"Der."

"Eddie say's that he's starving."

"What about all the rubbish in the caravan?" worried Scar.

"Well, it can't go anywhere, can it?"

"We'll clean it up later," decided Haemar. "Come on! He emptied what was left of their money into his pocket. It didn't take very long. And as Eddie was indeed hungry, it didn't take very long before the minibus was parked up outside a café in town, with a nice view of the lake through the rather dirty windows.

"Hey, look," said Felldyke. He pointed to one of the grimy windows. "There's a poster for the gig! Come on, this has to be a decent place ter eat." He pushed open the door, and the rest of The Banned followed him inside. All but one of the tables were unoccupied, and whilst Eddie and Haemar made for the counter, Scar and Felldyke started pushing other tables together. The noise did more to rouse the proprietor to emerge from the kitchen than Haemar's forceful attempts with the bell had managed.

"What's up with yer nose?" asked Haemar.

"Had a spot on it," replied the café owner, through the enormous bandage that covered half of his face.

"Oh, sorry."

"Do you have to move all the tables abut like that? What if someone else wants to come in?"

"No one ever seems to come in here recently," commented the only other customer, whose head was hidden by his dark hood. "And more tea!" he called. The proprietor looked distraught.

"Wotcher," Scar greeted the hooded customer cheerfully.

"Good day to you. Possibly."

"All right in here, isn't it? Do you come in here often?"

"Everyday, at the moment."

"Don't I know it," muttered the proprietor, and ducked.

Haemar looked at him curiously. "Are you all right, mate?"

"Yes, sorry. What can I get you?" asked the proprietor.

"Let's see, now. There's five of us, so we'll have ten full cooked breakfasts."

"Der."

"Yes, Eddie. And, five pots of tea, too. After that, we'll see."

The proprietor looked all around his café. His eyes widened a bit as he took in the sobering* shape of Dai the Dragon. Dai gave him a little wave, and then settled back in his chair.

*[And presently sober, too.]

GG looked at the quiet figure on the other side of the café.

"Excuse me," he called. "Don't I know you?"

"It's normally people asking us that," Scar said to Dai, who started laughing.

"If you do, you probably wish that you hadn't," was the reply to GG.

"No, I'm sure that we've met."

"If so, it would have been on business. I'm on holiday at the moment, and don't really want to talk about work."

"Oh, I can understand that," said GG cheerfully. "But go on, give me a clue."

"I normally only visit humans."

"Well, seems like yer made an exception for me, then!"

"Look, I've nothing against you, so why don't you let me drink my tea in peace?"

"Sorry, no offence. I was just trying ter be friendly. I mean, you're sat here in this dreadful town, all on yer own. Can't be that much fun."

"Well, you aren't far wrong there. And, I do have to come here every year for a week or so on business. But I did have a conversation a few days ago with a witch."

The Banned all looked round, interested.

"Bet it were Grotbags," muttered Haemar.

"No," replied the voice from inside the hood. "She said she was called Grizelda."

Haemar nodded. "That's her. We know her quite well."

There came the sound of breaking crockery from the kitchen, as plates fell to the floor. "Don't tell me she's coming in as well!" called the proprietor.

"No, don't think so," said Scar.

"Good!" came the voice from the kitchen. "And I hope that that bunch of layabouts on some poster she made me put up stay away too."

"Der!"

"Has your human friend got a speech impediment?" asked the cloaked customer.

"No. He's a roadie. All roadies end up like that."

"A roadie? So, you are musicians?"

"If they are, they're Banned!" yelled the café owner, amidst the scent of frying mushrooms and sausages.

"Yes, that's us," said Dai who had misheard him. "The Banned Underground."

"Do you know, it's been ages since I've heard live music. Mostly I just get to hear Noddy Holder yelling: *Merry Christmas Everybody*."

"We don't do that one," said Scar with a shiver.

"Tell you what, why don't you come over to the gig tonight? I'd give you a pass, but we haven't got any," invited GG.

"Well, thank you. I might."

"What did you say yer name was?" asked Scar.

"I didn't. But it's Notsanta."

There was a crash as the café owner dropped all the food-laden plates. Luckily, Felldyke had been watching the food rather than The Banned's new friend, and shoved a table in the way just in time. Eddie and Haemar marched him back into the kitchens, and came out with more plates and dishes of food.

"Not Santa?" asked Dai.

"Don't ask."

"Right," said Scar, deciding that he didn't want to know.

"We'll not leave yer name on the door then. But I'm sure you'll get in anyway," said Haemar.

"Well, yes. But it's much nicer when you've been invited!" said Notsanta, cheerfully.

"Our pleasure," mumbled Scar.

"Let's celebrate! More Tea, café owning person!"

"How long have yer been coming in here?" asked GG.

"Couple of weeks now, everyday," replied Notsanta.

"And you still don't know his name?" GG nodded towards the proprietor.

"Never bothered. He comes when he's called."

"I'll bet he does. Are you here for long, Notsanta?"

"My transport's just having its annual service, so I'll be here now until the end of the week."

The café owner banged fresh teapots down on the table. "You said that you'd move on this week! You promised!" he said.

Notsanta glared at him. "Do you want to be reminded of the promise you made? Didn't keep that, did you?"

The café owner retired, looking hurt.

"Listen," said Haemar a little later after breakfasts, "We need to go and rehearse."

Notsanta nodded.

"I mean, it's been lovely meeting you and all…"

"But you were hoping that we won't meet again? Or at least, not whilst I'm on business."

"Well, yes."

"No offence taken, I assure you. It's been nice to have a talk, to be honest. Very few customers seem to come in when I'm here. Now, don't worry about the bill, I'll take care of it," said Notsanta.

"Are you sure?" asked Haemar.

"Yes, of course. See you around. Or not, as the case may be."

"Well, thanks," "Cheers!" "Nice one!" "Der!" chorused The Banned on their way out.

As the door closed behind Eddie, the café owner came hurrying out of the kitchen after his retreating customers. "Oi!" he yelled.

"Calm down," said Notsanta. "I told them that I'd take care of it."

The café owner looked ashen.

"So, it was on the house," smiled Notsanta. "Think of it as your contribution to the arts."

Chapter Fifteen

The Watches and the Little Helpers were all somewhat weary when they eventually trudged through the welcoming door of the pub. On the way, they had chatted of this and that, with The Watches careful not to reveal their allegiance to the forces of Evil and The Dark Lord.

"What will you guys do now?" asked Jerry, as they all settled down with a drink whilst the landlord prepared breakfasts.

"Oh, we'll go into town and make our way home," said Ned, airily.

"Just wondered if you had fancied coming to the gig that's on tonight? Some mates of ours are playing locally."

"Who? And how do you know?" asked Mungo, confused.

"The Banned Underground are on."

"How on earth can you know that?" asked Fred in wonder.

"The poster on the wall there," pointed Jerry.

"We know Fungus and the boys," said Ned. "We all come from the same area. They're a great band. Have you seen them often?"

"Not really," said Jerry.

"Even I've heard of them," said the landlord, starting the delivery of plates and food. "Everyone round here is pretty excited. It's a bit of a surprise gig, but word has spread pretty fast and everyone who can is going!"

"Everyone?" asked Ned.

"Everyone!" agreed the barmaid, arriving with more drinks.

"We'll be sorry to miss it," Ned said slowly. "But, we'll have ter be on our way."

"Will we?" asked the junior, disappointed. He always enjoyed the gigs.

"Unfortunately, duty calls." Ned stood up, and headed towards the payphone on the bar.

The assistant assistant sighed.

"Well, we'll be there!" cried Jerry. "We missed the first half of the set last time, don't want to be disappointed again!"

"What about The Sleigh?" asked Boris in a whisper.

"Idiot will have it repaired inside a couple of days. He always does, it's in his contract or something."

"It was pretty badly knocked about," worried Fred.

"No worries," dismissed Jerry. "Cosmetic damage, most of it."

"Not like repairing lipstick though, is it?" said Boris.

Everyone looked at him with interest.

"And, how would you know?" asked Mungo.

Boris blushed. Without artificial aids.

"Right," said Ned, returning from his telephone conversation at the bar. "I've organised us a taxi ride to town. It's been nice meeting you guys, see you around, maybe." He waved at his assistants to join him.

"Christmas, probably," nodded Jerry.

Reluctantly, the junior wizard and the assistant assistant followed Ned out of the bar and across the car park towards the road.

"Where's the taxi then?" asked the junior.

"Be here in a moment. I just wanted a quick word in private first."

The assistant assistant looked worried. "Please don't tell us that you've got a cunning plan."

"Yes, of course I have."

The junior groaned.

Ned frowned. "Do not try and tell me that you've no faith in my plans!"

"Wouldn't dream of it, O Team Leader."

"You're the boss. We're just following yer orders."

Ned looked satisfied. "Right! So, what we've found out is?"

"That the Boss' credit card hasn't been cancelled yet, as it paid for breakfast?"

"That it were a long walk to freedom?"

"That most of the town are going ter see The Banned tonight!" exclaimed Ned.

"Except us," complained the junior wizard.

"Right!" said Ned.

"More's the pity."

"Listen," said Ned, "When everyone's at the gig, guess what we're going ter do?"

"Miss out?"

"Steal The Notsleigh. And then shoot off home with it to The Grey Mage, who will richly reward us!"

"Ah," said the assistant assistant. "I take it back, boss. That is a cunning plan!"

"So, we'll go and check out the garage, then find somewhere to hide up until it goes dark."

"Here's the taxi," called the assistant assistant.

"Right," said Ned. "Now, not a word about The Plan."

"What Plan?"

"Good!"

"No, I meant, what Plan?" asked the junior.

Ned shook his head, and they all piled into the taxi.

"Where to?" asked the driver.

"Just into town," replied Ned, and the driver set off, quite slowly. The fare meter flashed quickly, and added three pounds to the charge.

"You can go a bit quicker, and turn that meter off," ordered the assistant assistant from the back seat.

"Who do you think you are?" demanded the driver.

"Consumer Complaint Inspectors," sneered the assistant assistant.

The driver swallowed hard. "Sorry, sir. Where do you want dropping? Er, no charge, right? No hard feelings?"

"Well, you can drive us – slowly- past this industrial unit, then drop us at any café yer like in the town."

Ned nodded approvingly, and gave the taxi driver a stern look. Before too long, the taxi was cruising past a rundown Industrial Unit with a faded sign over the door, reading : Dwarfs R Us.

"Bit run down that," commented the assistant assistant as they drove slowly past.

"Yeah," said the taxi driver. "They've been there for years, but I've never seen many people go there. They must make some money somewhere though, because these units aren't cheap to rent. But where? I've no idea."

"Hum," said Ned, broodingly.

"Oh I see!" said the taxi driver, carefully executing a turn in the road and casually executing a passing frog. "That's why you are looking at them!"

"No one said we were looking at anyone," said Ned carefully.

"Well, a mate of mine did try and take some stuff there to be fixed. Wouldn't let him through the door, they wouldn't. And when he got the lawnmower back – cost an arm and a leg too, he said, he reckoned it went so fast that it was dangerous. The only time he fired it up, it mowed his lawn, his neighbour's, and gave two Retrievers and a cat a close shave before he managed to turn it off."

"What did he do with it?" asked the junior.

"Sold it to some guy who said he wanted to race it. He ended up as world champion, apparently."

"Oh well, we're not that bothered. Now, to a discreet café, please."

" Dim problem.* My cousin has a café that's been pretty quiet for a couple of weeks. That'll be discreet all right."

* [Welsh for 'No Problemo']* *

** [Which is 'Terminator' for 'No Worries]***

*** [Which is Australian for absolutely anything. Or indeed, everything.]

"Sounds OK to me. Let's go," agreed Ned.

The taxi drove off at a sensible, law-abiding speed. And eventually approached a café near the lake.

"Oh look," said the assistant assistant. "There's a poster for The Banned in the window."

"Yes," said the taxi driver, "I've heard that they are playing tonight. Are they any good?"

"Yes," said the junior. "I'm sick to be missing the gig."

"Oh right. I'll have to try and get tickets."

"Have you got any money?" asked Ned.

"Yes," replied the taxi driver, and slipped one hand into his pocket just in case he was about to be attacked.

"Fine," replied Ned, noticing what the driver was doing but interpreting it the wrong way, "then you'll be able to get in. Very non-discriminatory, those lads. Anyone with the money can get into the gig."

"Right, good," said the taxi driver and with a relieved flourish pulled up outside a rather dingy looking café with a view over the lake.

"Cheers then," said Ned, and The Watches climbed out of the taxi, which drove away perhaps a little faster than it should have done…to the delight and satisfaction of the Police Officer with the hand held speed gun stationed openly in full view behind a hedge a little way up the road. A fast-moving taxi made a change from calculating the average elapsed speed of the short-skirted passers by, and whilst less photogenic was more likely to be career enhancing.

Ned pushed open the door of the café, and nodded to the only other customer, who was hidden behind a newspaper. His black hood concealed what might otherwise have been seen of him.

The junior wizard and the assistant assistant slid onto two not overly comfortable chairs, whilst Ned ordered three teas.

"Quiet in here," he said easily to the café owner who was scratching underneath the bandage that covered his nose.

 The café owner gave a muffled sob. Uninterested, Ned carried the tray of teas back to the table.

"Right," said Ned.

"Do you have to keep doing that?" asked the junior.

"What do yer mean?"

"Well, every time you look like that, you say 'Right'."

"Right!" nodded the assistant assistant.

"Well, why are you blaming me?"

"Who else is there to blame fer what you say?"

"Well, I can think of someone. Blame him, not me."*

*[Everyone blames me. I'm used to it by now.]

"All right." The junior wizard sipped his tea and pulled a face. "If we've got to hang around in here for a while, at least the author could have given us some decent tea."

"And some scones," agreed the assistant assistant.

Ned sighed. "Not much chance of that. I'd better go and get them."

The newspaper rustled, loudly, but the owner didn't put in an appearance. Ned rapped loudly on the counter, until the much put upon café owner came out of the kitchen.

"Yes?" he asked wearily. "What now?"

"Look, this tea is awful," Ned complained. "Make us some fresh, and we'll have half a dozen of those scones. With some jam whilst yer about it."

"I'll have more tea, too, if you are making it," called Notsanta from behind his newspaper. "And this lad is right. The last lot was awful."

The café owner shook slightly and the bandage around his head shifted to obscure one eye, as well as his nose. He hurriedly pushed it back up across his forehead, and looked a little less like a pirate, and the improved vision was greatly to his benefit. With a quite unnecessary level of engine noise, what could be dimly perceived through the grimy glass as a Vespa pulled up outside the café. The rider raised what was clearly either a violin case or a guitar case, and the café owner (who watched 1930s gangster movies on his day off) dived under the counter.

Notsanta lowered his newspaper, and all the of The Watches shook their wrists slightly, to be sure that their arms were free in their sleeves. Ned glanced all around, and started to raise his right arm. The door swung slowly open, and a leather motorcycle boot came through, followed by the rest of the rider. Everyone froze at the vision. Into the cafe came a black leather catsuit clad (and unmistakeably female) dwarf, carrying a large guitar case. In the still silence she walked over to the nearest table, laid the guitar case carefully down, then removed her black helmet and shook out her long blonde hair.*

*[Look, I'm a fantasy author, right? So indulge me some fantasy.]

Her boots rang on the wooden floor as she strode over to the counter. "Tea, please."

"Right, right, right away," stammered the café owner. She stared arrogantly around the room, and Notsanta vanished back behind his newspaper. "What's the matter boys? Never seen a girl with a guitar before?" she asked.

"Since you ask, no," replied Ned, keeping his composure. Neither of this fellows seemed capable of speech, but Ned was fairly sure that no magical force had achieved that desirable aim.

"Well, I can see that you are all *very* pleased to see me," she purred.

"Please, join us," Ned said to her. (Notsanta mentally awarded him a lot of points for managing to keep his voice calm). The café owner appeared with a tray full of teapots, miraculously clean cups, and fresh scones.

"Thank you," said Ned. The café owner, looking rather flushed, retreated reluctantly behind the counter.

"I'd better introduce myself. My name is Freya."

"I'm Ned, these are my two assistants. We are Dark Wizards."

"Ned, I thought that we weren't supposed ter tell people that!" hissed the junior.

Ned gave Freya a keen glance, which she seemed to appreciate. "I suspect that she already knows."

Freya nodded. "Being a True Dwarf, I can tell these things." She relaxed, and released the top zip of her catsuit a little. Well, a little more than necessary, perhaps. Notsanta's newspaper rustled vigorously, and the assistant assistant took a swig of his hot tea, to help his temperature cool down.

"Most dwarfs we know," pointed out the junior wizard suspiciously, "wear chainmail and leather."

"But I am wearing leather. Everywhere."

The assistant assistant showered hot tea across the table at his colleagues, who would have preferred a cold shower at that point.

"You're married!" hissed the junior in his ear.

"So? I can admire the view, can't I?" hissed back the assistant assistant.

"And the guitar?" asked Ned, loudly.

Freya leant back and eased her shoulders. The assistant assistant sprayed hot tea across the table, soaking the junior's shirt. As the shouting started, Freya grinned at Ned. "It's a bass. I learnt to play years back, but haven't managed to find a permanent spot in a band. For some reason, they all seem to break up a few months after I join them."

"I can't imagine why," replied Ned, and started thinking.

"It can be terribly hard for a girl on her own," Freya said soulfully.

227

""I'm sure. Listen, my Boss could have some work for a girl with your talents."

"I've been offered opportunities like that before."

The assistant assistant choked, and the junior had to slap him on this back. Perhaps with a shade more force than was strictly required. And the use of the Heimlich Manoeuvre was perhaps excessive too.

"No," said Ned, blushing. "I meant he might well have a proper job you could help him with. For money. He's an accountant."

"Oh, that's different. I like accountancy. I've always been good with figures."

Ned ignored the renewed barrage of coughing, and gave Freya a couple of business cards, which she stowed away in a concealed pocket.

"I'll give him a call in a week or so," she said.

"So, what are you doing here anyway?" asked Ned.

"Well, I was just passing through, when I saw those posters. I've never seen The Banned Underground, and thought I'd give them a listen."

"Oh they're great!" enthused the junior, now in full control of both himself and the assistant assistant.

"Do you know them, then?"

"Well, yes," said Ned. "But not on the sort of terms where knowing us would get you in free, or backstage or anything."

"Well, I never have trouble getting backstage if I want to."

The assistant assistant found no difficulty in believing that.

Freya yawned, and zipped up her suit. Picking up her helmet, she smiled at Ned. "I'll give you a call then in a week or so about that job." She leant across the table to pick up her guitar, and the assistant assistant needed more first aid. The door swung shut behind her, and as the Vespa's engine revved hard, and departed, the temperature in the café slowly lowered. Ned gave the assistant assistant a long hard look.

"I reckon that we'd better take him fer a long walk around the lake," he said to his junior.

The junior wizard nodded, and they grabbed the still vacant assistant assistant and hauled him out of the door. The café owner looked after them a little wistfully.

"More tea!" demanded Notsanta.

Chapter Sixteen

Haemar gazed around the village hall approvingly. Whilst his vanity raged at him, for after some of the gigs they had played recently the venue was small, he felt really at home.

"Close to our roots," he said aloud.

"You've got your helmet on. No one can see your roots," replied GG.

"No, no, I understand what he means!" claimed Dai.

"That'll be the day."

"No, look," insisted Dai. "This is where bands start. Their roots. OUR roots. Playing to ordinary people in a hall where they can dance to the music."

"And pay a lot less," grumbled Scar.

"Dai's got it," agreed Haemar. "That's exactly what I meant. It may only hold a few hundred, but we can make this place rock!"

"The foundations are probably too dodgy to cope," grumbled Felldyke.

"Come on. I've not felt this enthusiastic fer ages. Eddie, get the gear. Let's set up, and run through a few numbers. Get the sound right, and we can get enough tracks down to satisfy Adam, his ants, and our contract terms."

"It's really trendy doing this too," said Dai.

"What, playing to almost no one?" asked Scar.

"The Stones have done it. Surprise gigs everywhere in small clubs! Lots of other top bands do it too, under false names."

"So that no one will ever know, probably."

"Come on, Scar, get into the spirit!"

Scar looked around morosely. "No spirits here. No beer either."

"You can have a drink later!" ordered Haemar. "Right now, go and help Eddie with the kit!"

"Der!"

Still grumbling, Scar wandered out to the minibus, followed by the rest of the Banned. Whilst Eddie and Felldyke set up the drum kit, GG and Dai started to mess around with the electronics and the microphones.

"Haemar!" yelled GG from underneath the table containing the mixing equipment.

"Yes?" Haemar called back.

"Can yer make some noise?"

Haemar dropped the two mic stands and three cymbals he was carrying. As the echoes dies away, GG emerged from under the table, vibrating gently.

"That might have been a bit much. Can you sing something instead?"

"What, acapella?"

"Don't know that one," called Dai, waving cables around.

231

"How about: *Only You?*"

"Anything really."

Haemar drew a breath, closed his eyes and started on the Flying Pickets' song. Dai and GG huddled around the mixing board, and were joined by Scar. Scar was promptly sent onto the stage, and started moving the mic stands around as directed by GG.

"Left! That's right. No, the other left. Forwards a bit...too far. Step back. And again. And a bit more, back again...oh, he's fallen off the back of the stage. Haemar, you can stop singing, Scar's swearing is all I need ter set the levels."

"You should have said that first. I could have jumped on his foot instead of singing all that."

"Never mind. Let's get the rest of the speakers out now, and then when they are connected, we can start."

"Hang on," said Felldyke slowly, "we can't start. Fungus aint here."

"That's true," agreed Dai.

Haemar sighed. "Listen lads, let's just get on and practise. I know Fungus isn't here, but Grizelda will deliver him here in time for the show. She promised."

"Is that enough?" asked Dai, but for once even Scar wasn't worried.

"Dai, if she said he'll be here, he'll be here."

"Wonder what she's doing with him?" said Dai.

There was a pause, and a lot of private, horrified, internal introspection. Then, they all shook their heads.

"No. Just, no."

"Fungus wouldn't. Would he?"

"Of course not."

"But he's green already. And you all know how she likes frogs…"

"Just NO!" Haemar defended his friend. "There will be a sensible reason. We'll know, when we hear it. Now, let's play!"

"What?"

"Well, how about er…"

"Start with *Gimme Some Loving*!" ordered Haemar.

"Well?" demanded Haemar, after a moment of complete silence.

"Haemar," GG answered, "Fungus blows the intro. We're counting him in. And out."

"Oh come on. What about *Sweet Home Chicago?*"

The Banned started. And stopped.

"It all sounds a bit thin, without the sax there in the mix," GG said finally.

Haemar sat down at the front of the stage.

"It's no good, is it?"

"It's not the same," agreed Scar.

"We just need it," said GG.

"What?" said Felldyke.

"Fungus of course!"

"Der."

"Yes, all right, Eddie. Not it, him."

"Well, his sax playing anyway," sighed Scar.

"Not his recent attitude though," Felldyke grumbled.

"Whoa, what's been going on?" asked Dai, perplexed.

"Fungus has been acting all funny recently," explained GG, whilst Haemar looked a bit downcast.

"Der."

"Yer right, Eddie. He's not been his usual self for ages."

"I think Grizelda might know that," said Haemar slowly.

"Why?" asked Dai.

"Well, she were very keen ter take him off last night."

"I just thought that she fancied him," said Felldyke.

"Der!"

"I agree Eddie."

"Nah, they're just good friends," Haemar answered.

"Do you really think that she'll have him back in time fer the gig?" worried Scar.

"Tell yer what," Haemar sounded exasperated. "Why don't you go and ask her then?"

"Der! Der!"

"No Eddie," agreed GG. "I wouldn't want ter do that either."

Dai changed the subject quickly. "That caretaker cleaned up in here OK, didn't he?"

"Yeah," agreed Haemar. "I must have overpaid him."

"Is there anything left in the Tour Bus?" Dai asked.

"Der."

"Right, well it's still three or four hours until the gig, so what are we going to do?"

"Down the pub!" replied Felldyke, who was feeling peckish after his exercise on the drum kit.

"What about me guitars? And the kit?" asked GG.

"I know, we'll leave someone here to look after it all," decided Haemar.

"Der!"

"No, Eddie, it can't be you. You've got ter drive."

"Der?"

"Well, it's always you because you're the only one with a license."

"Der. Der."

"Well, it would drive me bonkers too, but we're all stuck with it at the moment."

"I wouldn't mind learning," suggested Felldyke.

"Der!!"

"What did Eddie say to me?"

"He might struggle to get you on the Insurance," lied Haemar.

"Oh." Felldyke turned away, having lost interest.

"So, which of us is going to stay here and guard the kit?" asked Scar.

"You are!" all the others replied.

"Oh, all right. I'll just stop here whilst you lot have fun, then, shall I?"

"Lads?"

The front doors of the hall swung shut behind the retreating band members, and Scar pulled a face. As the Sprinter drove off, he sulked around the hall for a few minutes, then turned the power back on for his keyboard and started practising *Light my Fire*. He wasn't quite happy with his solo, yet. Becoming engrossed, he missed the rasping snarl of the Vespa pulling up outside. He paid little attention to the gentle opening of the front door, and the booted footsteps across the floor also failed to distract his rapt attention. The motorcycle boot, attached to a shapely, leather-clad leg, arriving on the side of his keyboard stand *did* however disrupt his concentration.

"You know, you are really quite good," purred Freya.

"Er, er, er," Scar replied.

Freya tossed her head, and her long blonde locks stroked Scar's cheeks, contrasting nicely with his furious blushing colour. "I'd love to come and see you all play tonight," she whispered close to his ear.

Scar plunged his hand into his pocket.

"Oooooo, is that a sheaf of musical notation? Or are you just pleased to see me?"

"Er, no," Scar replied uneasily. "It's a pass. Get you in free tonight, it will."

"Lovely. Well, I'll see you later then." Freya turned, and walked slowly out of the hall. Scar watched every step closely, then (with a somewhat unsteady hand) returned to the middle section of *Light my Fire*. Long damped fires inside him had started smouldering.

✱

The evening sky was becoming very dark as Ned led his two assistants across a field at the edge of the town.

"Boss, do you know where yer actually going, then?" asked the junior wizard.

"Good question," muttered the assistant assistant. As a professional taxi driver, he found a rural environment uncomfortable. And smelly. Unseen dangers lurked all around, and he kept stepping in some of them.*

*[Because they were unseen, of course.]

"Of course I do," replied Ned, annoyed. "And if I didn't, well I've got the SatNav, haven't I?"

The assistant assistant stopped. "Not that thing. It's useless in a town, what good would it be out here?"

The junior nodded his agreement. "And I'm not convinced that it weren't responsible fer us ending up with those Druids."

"Don't be daft," ordered Ned. "Look, I stole a town plan from that terrible café."

"How could you steal it? They were free!" objected the junior.

"Well, it sounds more in character if I say that I stole it. Anyway, I marked the place with an X."

"So did the cows in this field," grumbled the assistant assistant.

"How do yer know that they are cows? Might be sheep."

"Well, if they were, I wouldn't want to meet one."

"Come on, stop moaning," ordered Ned and he set off again across the field, followed by this reluctant aides. At one side of the field, some dark shapes stirred.

"Look," complained the assistant assistant, "I don't want ter be here."

"You signed up ter become a Dark Wizard."

"Yes, Ned, but I didn't know I'd have ter walk across big fields in the dark. Anything could live in them."

"It's a field, for Surdin's sake. What's going to live in it?"

"Them?" asked the junior wizard, accelerating past them at his best speed.

The assistant assistant looked back. Various dark shapes were racing across the field in their direction, with assorted snorting noises added for effect. He fled after the junior.

"Come back!" yelled Ned, preparing a fireball.

"There's the fence!" gasped the junior, beginning to flag.

"Where?" panted the assistant assistant at his shoulder.

"Ouch! Blast! Here!" replied the junior, running into the hard wooden fence.

The assistant assistant took the fence in one leap, and his wails of distress rose into the starry sky. The junior looked back. The dark shapes were very close. Starlight gleamed on teeth. He grasped the fence, hauled himself onto the top, and, carefully stepping on the assistant assistant, jumped over the barbed wire fence situated behind the wooden fence onto the lane beyond.

The three ponies that had been rather annoyed at the night-time intrusion into their field sniggered to themselves, and trotted back to their preferred resting place.

The assistant assistant slowly calmed down, and with the aid of the junior wizard unhooked the somewhat tattered remains of his trousers from the barbed wire fence.

"Where's Ned?" he asked as the two sat on the verge, waiting for their heart rates to return to normal levels.

"Who cares?"

"Well, I care. He might be hurt."

"How nice of yer to care," grumbled Ned, carefully – if stiffly- climbing the fence. As the moon rose and shed her soft light across the rural idyll, his assistants could see that he was covered in what they both hoped for his sake was mud.

"Just horses. Nothing ter be worried about," Ned said, and stalked off down the lane.

The other two dark wizards looked at each other.

"Who was worried?" they said in unison.

"Ned?" asked the junior a few minutes later.

"What?"

"Are we meant ter be still on this secret mission, like?"

"Why?"

"Because you're leavin' a trail of footprints, and well, other wet stuff."

Ned cursed. Once he started, it seemed to go on for quite a while, until he finally turned to his fellows. "Wait here a second!" he snarled, and slid amongst some trees near a small pond. When he returned, the (possibly) mud had largely gone. Ned set off without another word.

"Ned, are we meant ter be still on this secret mission, like?"

"What?"

"Well, you're leaving a trail of wet footprints now."

"Shut up."

"Yes, Ned. Sorry, Ned."

The footprints dried in the warm air, as the three dark wizards approached the industrial estate that was their target.

"Right!" said Ned. He pulled his colleagues closer to him, and lowered his voice.

"Boss, there's no one about. Why are you whispering?"

"Habit," replied Ned shortly. "Now, that unit there" – he pointed at a large industrial unit, looming against the night sky – "is our target."

"Right, boss." The junior stood up, and started to walk towards it. Ned pulled him back.

"Don't be so stupid. There's bound ter be security."

"Yes, that bloke what we met in the café were complaining about them. Said that they kept skiving off. So, they will all be off watching The Banned tonight," replied the junior wizard.

"Wish we were," muttered the assistant assistant.

Ned glared at him. "So, we go in carefully. Watch yer step, and follow me. Do what I do."

Ned stood up, and slowly walked towards the unit. The moonlight illuminated the Dwarfs R Us sign over the door.

"Do yer know what's good about following him?" asked the junior quietly.

"What?" replied the assistant assistant, equally quietly.

"Whatever's going ter happen will happen to him first."

"Works for me. That's leadership, that is."

Ned crept around the side of the unit, followed at a discreet distance by his assistants. The guard dog barked, loudly, from close by and Ned jumped sideways. Swearing softly, he climbed out of the pool of water, and shook frogspawn out of his boot.

"Do we have ter do that too, boss?" asked the junior.

Ned glared at him. The junior wizard was getting a bit too big for his boots, he thought. Something would have to be done about that – but not just now.

"Shut up, and follow me," he hissed.

At the door of the industrial unit, Ned carefully raised his hands, palms forward, and –without touching – went around the doorframe. "Simple closing spell," he mused. "Must be something else as well, though, I can sense it."

"What boss?" asked the assistant assistant, concerned.

"Don't know, yet."

Ned raised his hands again, and the doorway was outlined in green flames for a moment. The lock clicked. Ned felt inside his cloak, and pulled out an extendable staff. With that, he pushed the door gently open.

"Considering that these are dwarfs, you'd think that they would oil the hinges," grumbled the junior as the echoes died away.

"Yeah, it's inconsiderate to burglars," agreed the assistant assistant. He brightened. "Hey, maybe we could sue! I know this dodgy solicitor."

"Not exactly a distinguishing feature that, is it?" asked Ned as his hearing returned to normal. Carefully he probed the inside of the doorway with the staff. There was a loud snap, and the staff came back put, shortened by a good third of its length.

"Could have been you, that," Ned observed maliciously to the other two.

"Um. Yes, boss. Point taken."

"You mean staff taken," pointed out the assistant assistant.

"Point is, my staff weren't taken," observed Ned, and gingerly stepped inside. His staff followed, and the assistant assistant promptly fell over the now closed bear trap. Ned lifted the remains of his staff, and some light laid bare the inside of the unit.

"Good grief. People bring work here?" asked the junior, looking at the rows of broomsticks, each partly dismantled and on workstands around the walls. Workbenches stood everywhere, often with pizza boxes stacked on them. The assistant assistant fell on one with a glad cry, and started eating leftovers. Ned looked at him with astonishment.

"How can he do that?" he asked the junior wizard.

The junior swallowed his mouthful of cold pizza. "I don't know," he replied.

"I'm starved!" said the assistant assistant. "It's ages since we ate anything! Aren't you hungry, too, Ned?"

"Course I am. But look, all we've got to do now is get out of here, get home, and the Boss will treat us ter everything you can imagine at the best restaurant in town."

"What, in that swanky hotel by the lake?"

"You bet. Now, both of yer grab that cloth! And, PULL!"

The three dark wizards grabbed hold of the sacking over a dark shape on a set of ramps. They pulled. Then they clambered out from under the sacking, and gazed in awe at the gleaming black Notsleigh. The assistant assistant went to the lift controls, and slowly, with a hiss of escaping air, the ramp lowered the Notsleigh to the floor.

"Wow," said the junior, softly.

Ned walked round, running his fingers across the gleaming black coachwork. The assistant assistant jumped into the front seat, and started to examine the controls.

"Well?" asked Ned. "Do yer reckon that you can fly it?"

"Actually, it does look pretty straightforward. Power here, guidance controls here, I'm not sure what this stuff is for," replied the assistant assistant.

"Well, we'll sort it out as we go. Can yer get it started?"

The assistant assistant examined the controls again, and then cracked his knuckles. As Ned watched impatiently, he leant forward and pressed a button. There was a deep hum, a brief rumble, and the Notsleigh quivered. Ned climbed on board, and looked at the control panel.

"I'm not too sure about the guidance," muttered the assistant assistant. "It looks like there's a lot of predetermined locations and waypoints in here."

Ned smiled, and extracted the SatNav from his pocket. He plugged the USB lead into a port on the dashboard, and after a moment the SatNav began to power up. Words flashed across the screen, too quickly to read. Images blurred, then stabilised.

"Identifying location…" intoned the SatNav. "Please wait…"

The assistant assistant continued to examine the unmarked controls, whilst the junior, at Ned's urgings, started to hunt for the controls for the main door of the industrial unit. The assistant assistant gingerly moved a lever forward a notch. The humming deepened, and the Notsleigh rose slightly from the floor. A touch on a small joystick rising from the dashboard caused the Notsleigh to move slightly forwards. The assistant assistant smiled, but Ned – who had not been anticipating the move – was jolted and touched the first switch on a bank next to the SatNav by accident. There was a roar, and a small but perfectly formed missile shot out of a concealed hole at the rear of the Notsleigh, and the front wall of the unit disintegrated.

The dark wizards looked at each other in shock.

"You were only supposed to blow the bloody doors off," said the assistant assistant in awe. The junior, stood beside what had been the doors, with a control box in his hand, seemed beyond speech.

"Get in!" yelled Ned, recovering.

"*What do you think you are doing now!*" screamed the SatNav.

"Winning, for once," smirked Ned. He turned to the assistant assistant. "Get us out of here!"

The assistant assistant nodded, and seized the small joystick. Slowly, the Notsleigh backed out of the unit, and turned around. The assistant assistant reached for the power lever as the junior wizard scrambled aboard.

"*We are all so going to regret this!*" screamed the SatNav, frantically trying to close its systems down. Ned grimly pressed its screen controls, keeping it online.

"Shut down, and I'll give you to the Druids!" he snarled.

"*NNNoooooooooooooooooooo*" screamed the SatNav as, with a wild cry, the assistant assistant took the Notsleigh off the ground and powered into the night sky.

"Can't yer keep it straight and level?" snarled Ned a few minutes later.

"Yeah, remember there's no seatbelts, here in the back," agreed the junior wizard. He was presently lying flat on the floor, with his arms and legs wrapped around anything that looked secure.

"Sorry," panted the assistant assistant, fighting with the controls. "It feels like there's a preset route, and I'm trying to override it manually."

"Right!" said Ned, and thumped the SatNav as hard as he could.

"Now what? Do you know who's going to be coming after us this time?" demanded the SatNav.

"Just get yerself into the guidance system, and take us home!" ordered Ned.

"Have you any idea what you're asking me to do, here?" asked the SatNav.

"Yes. Take us home."

"Were it that simple…"

"Look. We're at 2000 feet over North Wales. Either you take us home, or yer over the side."

"You wouldn't do that to me, surely? Not after all this time?" pleaded the SatNav.

"Trust me on this, he would," said the junior, now trying to crawl under the front seats.

The SatNav sighed. "Here's some light music."

"Turn it off!" yelled three voices, for once united, over the intro to Slade's *Merry Christmas Everybody*.

"You sure?"

"YES!"

"Oh all right. Oh, It's quite dark in here. Ha. Hum. Well, well, well, who would have thought that?"

"What?" asked three voices.

"I'd have expected all this to be a bit more modern. Right, I can see that this flight had a pre programmed destination. But I can sort that out."

"Good," sighed Ned.

"Right," announced the SatNav, "I am now in control."

"Which bit of that is the good bit?" asked the assistant assistant.

"The bit that says you might actually get to where you want to go," replied the SatNav.

"That bit works fer me!" agreed the junior wizard, still out of sight.

The Notsleigh suddenly tilted, and climbed steadily.

"What were that for?" demanded Ned, as the junior wizard whimpered in fear.

"Crossing Mount Snowden," advised the SatNav. "If you passengers would like to look out to your left, you will see, well, three thousand feet of night sky below you."

The junior whimpered again.

"Shortly we will be passing the coast, en route direct to the Lake District."

"RAF Valley Base, this is Hawk Jet Victor Kilo One-Six.""Victor Kilo One-Six, Valley Controller. Go ahead, pass your message."

"Valley, Victor Kilo is on a night training exercise, now returning to base. Presently inbound from the South, ten minutes to run, height 3000 feet."

"Victor Kilo, we have your radar trace. Be aware, we are tracking some unidentified local traffic in your immediate vicinity, no height information."

"Valley, this is Victor Kilo. Negative contact…wait one…confirm visual sighting of the traffic."

"Victor Kilo, Valley. Can you identify the traffic?"

"Valley, this is Victor Kilo. Not telling you…"

"Ha," yelled Ned triumphantly, as the fighter jet slid away below them. "Compared to this baby, even fighter jets are like dinosaurs!"

"Was it a 'Doyouthinkhe sauros' then?" came a voice from below the seats.

Ned deliberately bounced hard on his seat, and smiled at the cry of pain, then turned to watch the lights of the towns and cities on the coast pass by as the Notsleigh flew North. "The Grey Mage is going ter be pleased with us this time," he said happily.

Chapter Seventeen

The caretaker stood at the open doors to the village hall, watching the happy throng collecting inside the hall. The noise was louder than he remembered from the happy days of political meetings, where the audience could often be counted on the fingers of one hand.

"Tell me," he said to Eddie as the roadie stood guard over the takings, "is it a good life as a roadie?"

"Der."

"Oh."

"Der."

"I see."

"Der, der!"

"That as well? Oh well, I'm probably better off here, then."

"Der."

"And, as you say, there's no room in the tour bus."

"I'm sure that you would be able to find room for me if you tried." Freya gave Eddie a sweet smile and the pass she had conned out of Scar, before joining the rest of the audience.

"Der!"

"Yes, I can see that there are compensations. Right, I'd best go and swill out the toilets again."

Eddie closed the heavy bag, and nodded to Fred and Boris who were sat on chairs nearby. They were acting as his security tonight. The three made their way through the crowd to the backstage area, and handed the bag over to Felldyke before going back out to the mixing desk.

As they left, the doors were pushed open, and a number of policemen in full uniform entered the hall. The sergeant gave his orders, and they spread out around the room.

"Sarge?" asked one young PC.

"Yes lad?"

"Is there any catering here then?"

"Don't think so, lad, why?"

"Oh, I thought ice creams were traditional, that's all. I just fancied an orange one."

"Dream on, boy, dream on."

"I thought that we had come here to arrest them all on suspicion, Sarge."

"Suspicion of what, lad?"

"Impersonating musicians, for a start!"

"If we were going to arrest people for that we'd have a permanent stand at those TV Talent Show auditions."

"Be a better posting than this town, Sarge."

"Shut up."

Behind the curtain strung across the back of the stage, similar sentiments were being expressed.

"In yer dreams!" worried Scar.

"Look, there's ten minutes before we are due on. She'll be here," said Haemar. He then lay down, filled his mouth with water, and started gargling.

"What if he doesn't get here?" demanded Scar.

"Then we play without him," said GG from inside an amplifier.

"How?"

"Fer heaven's sake, Scar, we'll manage. Felldyke can go on and do a drum fill to open and set us up, and we'll just busk it from there. Like the old days."

"What old days?" asked Dai, tuning his bass guitar.

"Oh, any old days," replied GG, and vanished back into the amplifier.

In front of the stage, the audience were starting to sound impatient. Cries of "We want The Banned!" started intermittently. Haemar spat out the water, and rinsed his mouth with whisky to get rid of the taste. Felldyke pushed a last drumstick into his stage smock, which already bristled with them, and picked up the wooden drumsticks. The chanting started to intensify as the hands of the clock over the stage reached nine pm.

"Well," said Haemar reluctantly, "looks like I were wrong. I hate being wrong. In fact, I can't remember the last time I were wrong."

"We can," GG assured him, picking up his Les Paul.

"Tell you what, I'll go on and start a drum intro, and you lot can follow as and when yer like," suggested Felldyke.

Somewhat tense, the rest of The Banned agreed. To enormous applause, Felldyke lumbered onto the stage, climbed up behind the drum kit and raised his sticks. Behind him, Haemar and Dai lifted the bag of takings onto the stage and fastened the chain around their drummer's leg. Felldyke raised his drumsticks above his head, and in a rare moment of silence, brought them crashing down.

Haemar poured a can of beer over his scarf, and wrapped it around his wrist. "Usual start, then into *Gimme Some Lovin*," he ordered. "Dai, you know that riff?"

"Yes, Haemar, of course," replied the dragon a bit affronted. He snorted, and the flames blew across the stage, to cheers from the crowd. The caretaker came running around a corner brandishing a small fire extinguisher, and stopped, perplexed.

"Then, you can lead us in," said Haemar grumpily, after putting out his eyebrows with his damp towel. He turned, and strutted out onto the stage, followed by Scar and GG

"Just keep the flames down," grumbled the caretaker as Dai bounced past him.

"Here we go!" yelled Haemar into the mic, and The Banned drove straight into *Going Underground*, to a lot of applause.

"Hit it, Dai," howled Haemar, as he came to the end of the song, and Dai duly started the famous *Gimme Some Loving* riff, with GG sliding in after him on the Les Paul guitar. Scar started counting for his entry, and lost count (and his balance) at a wild blast of sound from the rear of the hall. The doors flew back, with quite unnecessary theatricality, and in bounced Fungus followed by Grizelda and the vampires.

"Will you look at Fungus!" yelled Dai to GG as he pulled the guitarist out from underneath Scar.

"Will you listen to him!" screamed Haemar his expression transformed in delight. All eyes turned to look at the wild saxophonist, who was being pushed towards the stage on a wheeled trolley, two of the vampires providing the motive power. Dai was truly amazed, and his flames flickered out across the stage and rose into the roof. He had last seen Fungus as a dingy green colour, with a strange waistcoat and grey baseball cap. Now, the BogTroll shone with a luminescence capable of lighting up the whole stage (and the caretaker duly scurried off to dim the lights further as a power saving measure), and he was blowing a real storm on the sax.

Carried along by the rejuvenated presence of their leader, The Banned poured their hearts and souls into the set. Eddie was frantically working the mixing desk, and cursing steadily as he tried to control the levels for the tape machine. The crowd were going wild.

"Interval," gasped Haemar after forty minutes. Fungus nodded at Grizelda, who unsurprisingly had been able to get to the front of the crowd quite easily, and the witch promptly threw a whisky bottle at Haemar, who caught it in a reflex action.

"Sing!" demanded Fungus, and broke into *Please don't go*. Haemar looked at GG, who shrugged and joined the riff. Felldyke was sweating so much that he had discarded his smock, and Scar's keyboards were smoking.

At last even Fungus had had enough, and the show closed to *Johnny B Goode and Jailhouse Rock*, favourites of both The Banned and the audience, who eventually left, well satisfied.

"Good set that, lad," sighed the Police Sergeant.

"Do we arrest them now, Sarge?"

"No," suggested Notsanta, emerging from the crowd.

"Excuse me, Sir, this is technical police business. Move along."

Notsanta moved along, but only after whispering something into the sergeant's ear.

"Sarge?"

"SARGE!"

"Oh, what? Er, yes, get the lads out of here. Quick!"

"Sarge? Aren't we supposed to be asking questions, Sarge?"

"I've just had all the answers I need!"

"Oh. Cor, look at her on that Vespa. Wow."

The Vespa revved up, and left the car park, the smooth leather catsuit having grown some unsightly lumps, the size of two cassette tapes.... Backstage, The Banned clustered around Fungus.

"Man, just look at you," enthused Haemar. "What did she do to you?"

"It were simple," said Grizelda quietly. "You've all been working so hard this last two years that yer forgot something important."

"What?" asked GG, carefully.

"To look after your boss!" exclaimed Grizelda dramatically. In tribute to the strength of their friendship, Haemar chose not to take issue at that point with the word 'Boss'.

"What do yer mean?" Scar asked into the silence.

"Fungus is a BogTroll. Every so often he needs to spend a little time in a bog."

"Don't we all?" asked Felldyke.

"Is that what yer did with him?" asked GG.

"Yes. I buried him," Grizelda smirked.

"We had been worried about that," confessed Dai.

"I found a bit of bog nearby to my mobile home, and covered him over for a day. It's what he needed. Look at the difference."
Indeed, Fungus was clearly rejuvenated from the jaded, grumpy mood he had been in a couple of days earlier, although now he was lying on his back, cradling his sax lovingly.

"True. He were on fire, tonight," agreed Haemar.

"On fire! On fire!" echoed the caretaker rushing in.

"How would you know?" asked Scar, slightly affronted.

Eddie too came in. "Der! Der!" he yelled, and ran out again. The Banned looked at each other confused.

"Fire, you idiots!" yelled the caretaker again, and rushed out. Dai sent a small blast of flame after him, but he was tired, and missed.

"Der!" yelled Eddie again, putting his head round the curtain.

Haemar looked confused, and walked up to the curtain that formed the backstage area. He peered around, and then flung it back.
"Fire!" he yelled.

"What at?" asked Dai, lazily, blowing smoke rings.

"Get the kit out! The place is on fire!" yelled Haemar.

The Banned were galvanised.

"Each get yer own kit first!" yelled Haemar.

"Who's got the money?" demanded Fungus, waking up fast.

"I'll need help with the drumkit," shouted Felldyke, as the flames started to lick around the stage.

"Der!"

"Has Eddie got the desk and tapes?" shouted Haemar through the confusion, as smoke rose all around.

"What?" called Scar, staggering back in through the door.

"Has Eddie got the desk and tapes?" repeated Haemar.

"I got the desk out!" called Scar.

"We moved the drum kit," shouted Grizelda, smoke pouring from her hat, as she sat beside Santa's Little Helpers.

"Where are those vampires?" asked Dai, looking around.

"Oh, they had to run fer it, can't get near to fire, it's a bit fatal for them."

"But not for us?" asked GG as part of the roof fell in, and the flames roared higher.

"Hands up who hasn't got the sense that they were born with," called Fungus opening the door.

"What do yer mean?" called back Haemar.

"Run for it before the rest of the roof goes!" yelled back Fungus.

"He's right, really," agreed Dai.

"I suppose that you are right at home here," observed GG, looking around at the blazing ruin of the village hall all around them.

Dai looked confused. "No, I live on the south coast. I'm a stranger here myself."

The Banned staggered from the fire, and collapsed against the side of the Sprinter. In the near distance, they could hear the sound of sirens as the Fire Service raced to the rescue.

"That's wrong," observed Fungus.

"Yeah," agreed Dai.

"Der der der, der der, der der," said Eddie.

"Der der der, der der," agreed Dai.

Haemar started laughing, and Fungus reached for the sax.

As the firemen turned into the car park, they were treated to a spirited rendition of *Smoke on the Water*.

"You trying to be funny?" demanded the Fire Chief.

Jerry walked up to him and whispered in his ear. The Fire Chief went a funny colour, and sat down hard. One of his men hurried up, but the Fire Chief waved him away.

"Listen," Mungo said to The Banned, "we're off now."

"Oh, right. Well, I hope you enjoyed the gig," said Fungus happily.

"Scorcher," commented Fred.

"Anyway, can you lot be at Caernarfon airfield tomorrow night?" asked Mungo.

The Banned all turned to look at Eddie. Eddie kicked the bag with the takings.

"Der," he nodded.

"That's a 'yes', then," agreed Haemar.

"Good. We'll pick you up then in The Sleigh, and we'll have a gig at the Grotto organised."

"I thought that The Sleigh were a wreck?" asked GG, confused.

"Oh, Idiot will have got it sorted by now. He always does, it's in his contract," said Fred easily.

"So, what is it that you are going ter do?"

"Well, we'll go and see the Vampire Mechanic with these other vampire gentlemen, and then bring The Sleigh away. We'll have to take it for a test flight tomorrow so that we can complete the paperwork and approve release of the monies for the work, and that's when we'll pick you up."

"Just like that?" asked Scar.

"Just like that," agreed Boris, feeling relieved.

"The gig is set up, just like we promised," said Jerry, coming round the side of the tour bus. "We owe you, big style, for helping us. So. Maybe this gig will repay our debt. Not many get to say that they've played Santa's Grotto."

"Jerry," hissed Boris, "What about the power?"

"No worries!" Jerry replied, "we'll put a couple of the reindeer in the old treadmill, and wire it up to the generators!"

With a wave, the four Little Helpers walked off into the night with the vampires.

"Tell me, " Jerry asked the Count as they left, "what's it like being Undead?"

The Count looked bitterly at his two colleagues who were wandering off ahead of them. "Just as annoying as it was being alive. Only it lasts longer. Take my tip, don't try it."

"Will they be safe?" Scar asked Grizelda.

"Oh, yes. I told the Count that if they touched yer mates, I'd be coming looking for him..."

GG shuddered. "That should do it."

Grizelda chuckled.

"You're in a good mood," Haemar said carefully.

"Yes. Me contract is finished, and I can go back to Ben, me husband. I'll be glad ter get home."

"Um."

"I'm just going ter pack up the stuff in the mobile home, then I'll be away." Grizelda yawned, and picked up her broomstick.

"See you guys next time," she called, and wobbled off unsteadily into the night.

The Grey Mage walked carefully around The Notsleigh, with his mouth wide open. "Ned, I have to accept that this time you have actually fulfilled your instructions," he said.

"Does that mean that we get the bonus, Boss?"

"Not only that, but I'll accept the expenses that you put on that credit card."

Ned smiled, but the assistant assistant looked worried. The Grey Mage noticed, and smiled. "Tomorrow, get yourself round the local garages, and order a replacement for that Mondeo taxi," he said.

The assistant assistant gave a broad smile. The Grey Mage climbed into the front seat of The Notsleigh. "Talk me over the controls," he asked.

"Right, Boss," agreed the assistant assistant. "Now there seem ter be three banks of the flight controls."

"I see."

"These on the right are the actual flight controls, around this small joystick."

The Grey Mage put a finger on the joystick, and wiggled it. Ned twitched, but nothing happened.

"This bank in the center seem ter be for a guidance system. Ned over rode it by attaching that SatNav, for us ter get home."

"Smart thinking, there, Ned!" approved The Grey Mage.

"Thanks, Boss. According to the SatNav, none of it started up until we went higher than 2000 feet, so probably there's some sort of safety cut out."

"I see. And those on the left?"

"We didn't try them out, Boss. Well, except for one, by accident like. It seems to be for an onboard weapons system."

"A weapons system?"

"Yes, Boss. Ned tried one, by accident, and it blew the front off an industrial unit."

The Grey Mage snatched his hand away from that part of the instrument panel as if he had just been bitten by an adder. "A weapons system," he said again, and started laughing.

"What's funny, Boss?" asked Ned.

"Well, old Skinner who runs our coven at the moment, he sent his acolytes South, and all they came back with was an old James Bond Aston Martin."

"What's funny about that, Boss?"

"Well, they stole one for him with those machine guns in the front wheel arches, and trailered it back North on a low loader. He tried it out two days ago."

"And?"

"No one had told them that with the guns onboard, it could only drive in a straight line.* He set off up the motorway, and he had to drive for nearly two hundred miles before he found enough people to pick it up, and turn it round by hand, so that he could go home. This, *this*, is going to blow them all away."

*[True. Look it up online if you don't believe me.]

Ned smiled.

"Well might you smile, Ned, for our advancement in the craft is fully assured with this. Now, when shall we try it out?"

"Well, boss, it's getting light now. Someone is bound to notice if we go fer a spin."

"Why," suggested the assistant assistant, "don't we go for a spin tomorrow evening, when it's quiet? We can try it out properly, and nobody's going ter see us."

"Good idea," agreed the junior wizard. "We could go over one of the valleys, and try the weapons."

"And if we are seen," mused The Grey Mage.

"Easy, Boss. The farmers will just think we are another UFO and ignore us. Of course, we might have ter shoot down the odd UFO."

"Just like Space Invaders, eh?" laughed the junior.

"Now, that takes me back," said The Grey Mage. "I used to play that in the pub."

"You always used to cheat, too Boss. That's why they banned you."

"I know. Shame, it was a useful addition to the office petty cash. One evening a week paid for all the tea bags and milk."

"Couldn't you just go to a different pub, Boss?"

"No, word got round that I was unbeatable and they all told me that I was invading their space."

The Grey Mage walked around The Notsleigh again, entranced. At the rear, he paused to examine the ports and slots of the weapons systems. His staff held their breaths, but nothing violent happened.

"And it doesn't need reindeer?"

"No, Boss. We flew up here without any worries."

"So, what does it use for fuel, I wonder?"

"Don't know Boss. But I bet that we could find out online."

The Grey Mage smiled. "True. Wikipedia seems to have an answer for everything."

"I thought that were Einstein?" asked the junior wizard.

"A very wise man, that," agreed Ned.

"Wasn't he into relatives?" asked the assistant assistant with a smirk.

"Only in theory."

"Right," said The Grey Mage decisively. "It's almost time to open the office, so let's get to work and meet here again at sundown." He pushed the others out of the rented garage, and locked the door.

"I did think that we might have the day off," suggested Ned.

"We have to think of appearances, Ned," reproved The Grey Mage. "Staff will be wanting a day off on account of being ill, next!"

"Or dead, even," said Ned a trifle sarcastically.

"Oh, I'd let them off if they were dead. Unless they applied in person. Then I'd have to relocate them within the practice and hold them to their employment contracts."

"The Undead? You'd keep them working?"

"Of course," replied The Grey Mage, surprised. "Lots of

accountancy practices only survive because the audit staff are zombies."

"How do you apply the Health and Safety Regulations to them?" asked the junior, eager for knowledge.

"Braaaiiiiinnnssss," The Grey Mage answered.

"Right," said Ned.

"Come on." The Grey Mage led his staff towards the office. "I'll stand you all a decent evening meal before we take it up for a test flight."

"When's the next Coven meeting, Boss?"

"Tomorrow night. If we check out OK on it tonight, then we'll fly in to the Coven. That'll wipe the smiles off a few faces!"

Chapter Eighteen

The Sprinter was negotiating the last of the assorted roundabouts on the way out of the town, when Haemar's attention was drawn to a figure on the side of the road, waving at them.

"Do we know him?" he asked loudly.

"Never seen him before," replied Fungus, taking a brief glance before returning his attention to the stack of CDs.

"Der."

"You're right, Eddie. He *was* in the café."

"What café?"

"You missed it, Fungus," Haemar said, looking out of the window again.

"Der."

"No, I know that it was worth missing. Fungus probably had more fun being buried alive."

"Der."

"Shut up. And stop."

"Der?"

"We'll squeeze him in somewhere. On top of Felldyke, probably."

As the drummer was now deeply asleep, he was not in a position to complain or object, so Eddie pulled over. Without a word, the hitch hiker climbed in, and settled down between Felldyke and Scar.

"Wotcher," greeted Scar. "You're the one who isn't Santa, right?"

"Right," agreed Notsanta, sitting down.

"Not santa?" asked Fungus, confused.

"Don't ask," said Notsanta.

"Well, can I ask what you want?" asked Fungus.

"Of course," replied Notsanta.

There was a pause.

"Well?" asked Fungus.

"Well? You asked. Didn't say that I was going to answer."

"Of come on. You're in our tourbus, you have no idea where we're going."

"Sorry," interrupted Notsanta, "but of course I know where you are going."

"But it's a secret!" objected Haemar.

Notsanta looked at Haemar from underneath his cowl, and Haemar decided not to pursue his questioning. In case he got an answer.

"Jerry and Mungo are picking you up," said Notsanta.

"Yes," agreed Scar nervously. "That's right."

"Then you'll be going to The Grotto."

"Well, yes," agreed Scar, still nervous.

"So, I'll hitch a ride."

"Why would you want to go to The Grotto?" asked Dai.

"Maybe I fancy seeing you lot play again."

"No offence, Mr-who-isn't-Santa, but The Grotto?"

"It's home," admitted Notsanta.

"The Grotto?" asked Haemar.

"Yes. Does your driver know the way?"

"Der."

"Der?"

"He's got directions," explained Haemar.

"I seem to have missed quite a bit in one day," mused Fungus.

"Er, well, we did get a bit busy," agreed Haemar.

"And, we seem to have missed quite a bit in the money bag."

"Ah. Well. You see..." started Haemar.

"Well, we had this sort of party," added Dai.

"A party? For how many?" demanded Fungus.

"Just us, really."

"But that bag had the fee from the Big Gig!"

"Well, yes. But it were a good party, Fungus. You would have enjoyed it."

Fungus shook his head. "How are we going to make it if you lot keep drinking what we earn?"

"We'll get by," muttered Haemar, and he pulled his helmet over his eyes.

Fungus turned on the CD player.

"What's that?" asked Haemar, from underneath his helmet.

"Seasick Steve. *I started out with nothing, and I've still got most of it left.*"

Eddie drove on, in an injured silence.

"Sorry, Fungus," said Haemar quietly.

"Oh, forget it. Hey, have you got those tapes from the gig? Let's check them out!"

"Good idea! Hey Scar, have yer got the tapes?"

"What tapes?" asked Scar.

"The ones we recorded at the last gig!" said Haemar.

"I thought that you had them, or Eddie."

"Der!"

"No Eddie," said GG, "I haven't got them."

"Then who has?" asked Haemar.

There was a silence.

"Great!" complained Fungus. "I take a day off, and you spend all the money and lose the live tapes!"

"We were busy getting the kit out of the fire," GG retorted.

"Those tapes would have bought us new kit!"

"Well, I got the mixing desk," said Scar. "It's in the back. Maybe the tapes are in there too?"

GG twisted round, and managed to crawl into the rear load area. "There's one tape here, in the equipment," he called over his shoulder.

"Der!"

"Yes, Eddie, I know that there should be three," agreed Haemar.

"Can't see any more, but it's a bit dark here."

"Do you want some more light?" asked Dai.

"NO!" yelled The Banned quickly, and Dai pulled a face.

"They must have gone, in the fire," sighed Scar.

"Not underneath Felldyke are they?" asked GG hopefully.

Dai prodded Felldyke hard with one talon, and Scar checked as Felldyke leapt into the air.

"No," reported Scar, as Felldyke landed and the Sprinter shook from the impact.

"Worth a look, though," sighed GG.

"What?" asked Felldyke. "Why didn't yer just ask me?"

"Der."

"Yes, Eddie, we'll not do that again."

"Two tapes worth," sighed Fungus.

"Never mind," GG called, trying to climb back into his seat. "We'll get some more at this next gig."

"Right," agreed Haemar, and closed his eyes.

Before long, Eddie drove onto the airfield, close to the sea wall. The wind blew strongly, and the grey seas heaved and crashed on the stones, throwing plumes of spray into the air, and down onto the tour bus.

"Here? Really?" asked Scar, disbelievingly.

"Yes," replied Notsanta, who had been very quiet. "Here."

"Why here, fer heaven's sake?"

"Well, it's quiet."

The wind howled, and the Sprinter rocked as a wave lashed across the sea wall into the side of the tour bus.

"Isolated," continued Notsanta.

The Banned looked out of the side windows at the motley collection of VW Campervans painted in various bright colours.

"Just as well that those surfboards are tied to the roof bars. Any lower and those vans would be floating," said Scar.

"Discreet," added Notsanta.

"*Discreet?*"

"Well, no one is going to believe any of that lot if they run round saying that Santa's Sleigh turned up and collected a bunch of musicians, are they?"

The Banned looked at each other, lost for words.

"Der. DER. *DER!!!*"

"What's going on?" yelled Haemar, as the tour bus rocked more violently than before and suddenly lifted off the ground. All heads twisted round at a loud knocking on the driver's window, then twisted round further as Mungo's grinning face appeared – upside down – outside. Eddie opened the window.

"Going up," said Mungo. And went up, out of sight. So did the tour bus, to assorted cries of alarm, or indeed, panic.

"Relax," shouted Notsanta over the din.

"What do yer mean relax?" yelled Scar, looking out of his window at the churning, frothing sea below. "Why would I relax?" Several clouds drifted past, also below his window.

"Well, how did you think that we were going to The Grotto?"

The Banned looked at each other, and started to calm down a little.

"We are in The Sleigh's transporter field now, all the way home," Notsanta explained.

"Your home maybe. I thought that we weren't going ter see ours again!" grumbled Scar.

"Ned, you can go and pay," said The Grey Mage.

"Me, Boss? Thought that you were paying for the meal!"

"Use that credit card that I gave you. I'm sure that you've used it before."

"Er, mebbe once or twice."

"A night, I think. I see the entries online, you know."

The two junior wizards swallowed. "It were him!" they said in unison, pointing at Ned, who glared back at them.

"Go on, then we'll go on our mission," The Grey Mage said.

"Yes, Boss," chorused the junior and the assistant assistant.

"And discuss the expenses later."

"Yes, Boss."

"Right," said Ned, a few moments later. "All done."

His face alight with anticipation, The Grey Mage led the way out of the curry house, and along the street to the rented garage. Unlocking the doors, he also released the spells he had placed on them for protection.

"Just as well no one tried ter force their way in here," said Ned.

"Yes. We'd have heard the screams in the office," replied The Grey Mage cheerfully.

The assistant assistant swallowed.

"You can reverse it out here for me, then I'll try her out," The Grey Mage said to him.

The assistant assistant swallowed. Again. Then carefully climbed into the front of The Notsleigh, and looked again at the controls. He selected the power controls, and shortly afterwards, there came a loud humming noise, and The Notsleigh rose an inch or two into the air. Very, very carefully, the assistant assistant reversed it out of the garage, and turned to face down the length of the lane.

Beside himself with excitement, The Grey Mage leapt aboard, and took the controls.

"Get in the back, you two!" he ordered, and Ned and the junior wizard climbed, rather hesitantly, into the back. Out of sight of The Grey Mage, the junior produced two long leather belts. Ned grabbed one with a grateful look, and the two strapped themselves to secure points in the back.

"Here we go," exulted The Grey Mage, and seized the joystick. The Notsleigh trembled, and as the power lever was pushed firmly forward, moved smoothly along the lane, and then soared upwards into the dark sky. "Wow!" yelled The Grey Mage. "Wait until the guys see us arrive in *this*! Control of the coven will be ours in hours!"

"Boss," yelled Ned from the back seat, but his voice was whipped away by the wind of their passage, as was the wind of the assistant assistant's passage.

The junior wizard twisted towards him. "How high are we, Ned?"

"Too high," Ned replied grimly. "I didn't bring the SatNav!"

The Notsleigh lurched, as the guidance unit fought the joystick for control of their flight path...and won.

"What's going on?" cried The Grey Mage. He struggled again with the joystick, and it came off in his hand. With a snarl, he tossed it overboard.

"We've gone over 2000 feet!" shouted the assistant assistant.

"So?" demanded his coven leader.

"The automated guidance systems have cut in. Ned did tell yer, Boss."

"Did he? When?"

"Page 260, Boss."

"Oh. In writing?"

"Someone's writing, yes."

"Oh. Ah well, my mistake then. Where's the SatNav, Ned?"

"Um, it refused to come, Boss. Something about Prescient Predictive Programming."

"So you mean that we are stuck here, going where ever this Notsleigh decides to take us?"

"Yes, Boss."

"Remind me to have a staff appraisal meeting with you when we get back. The electric cattle prod will make a good staff to appraise you with."

"Boss, can you over rule the guidance systems with yer magic?" asked Ned.

"Let's see, shall we?"

The Grey Mage raised both his hands over the flight computer, and started muttering. His muttering swelled to a chant, as coloured lights flashed between his hands and the computer. His chant rose to a roar, as he poured all of his power at The Notsleigh: which flew on regardless. The Grey Mage slumped back in his seat, exhausted.

"Oh well, suppose we might as well sit back and enjoy the ride."

"Hey guys, look over there!" shouted the assistant assistant.

"Why? What is there to see beside clouds?" asked the junior wizard.

"Look just below those clouds! First, there's a jet fighter!"

"Oh great! First we lose control of this thing, then the RAF turn up!" howled The Grey Mage.

"And, beyond that, there's another Sleigh!"

"He's right," agreed the junior wizard. "And that must be Santa's, because look! There's the reindeer!"

"And what's that under it?" asked Ned, slowly.

The rising moon gleamed a soft light onto the dangling tourbus.

"That's The Banned!"

"And, it looks like their might be going where were going!" agreed the junior wizard.

"Excellent! Maybe there will be a gig, and we can bum our way in!" The assistant assistant was excited at the thought.

"But what about the fighter?" asked Ned slowly.

"Victor Kilo One Six, Fighter Control. Radar traces merged. Are you visual on the targets?"

"Fighter Control, Victor Kilo. Contact acquired."

"Victor Kilo, Fighter control. Identify intruders."

"Victor Kilo, Fighter Control. Repeat, Identify intruders."

"Victor Kilo, Just what's going on up there?"

"Fighter Control, Victor Kilo. Even I don't believe this one, so I'm taking photos on my phone as proof!"

"Victor Kilo, Fighter Control. Just get back here, now, will you? And this time the explanation had better be a good one!"

"The jet's turning away, Boss!"

"Well, at least that's one less thing to worry about, then."

Some time passed in silence.

The assistant assistant was poring over the flight controls, and messing about with the GPS device on his phone. "Boss, We must be getting close to the ice pack now."

"You reckon?" asked Ned.

Then the Notsleigh suddenly started to lose some height.

"We're following the Banned on the same course, and keeping at the same height as them, Boss. We're obviously going ter the same place."

"Wherever that is," said The Grey Mage, grimly.

"Losing height fast, Boss," continued the assistant assistant.

"Boss?"

"What?"

"We'll soon be at 2000 feet over the snow cap."

The Grey Mage looked at the assistant assistant. "So?"

"Then, we'll be below 2000 feet over the snow cap, Boss."

"And your point is?"

"That we go back to manual control Boss. Have yer still got that joystick thing?"

"You mean that bit that came off in my hand?"

"Yes!"

"No."

"Oh."

"Hey, er Notsanta?" Scar nudged the sleeping shape on the seat next to him until Notsanta woke up.

"Are we nearly there yet?" asked Notsanta

The Banned all looked at him speechless.

"How would we know?" asked Haemar.

"Um. Yes. Right."

"Hey, look, is that yer Notsleigh behind us?" asked Scar.

"I expect so," replied Notsanta without looking. "It's programmed to return to base if it takes to the air without me."

"So, who's going ter be in it?" asked GG.

Haemar and Fungus looked at each other, and started laughing.

"What's funny?" asked Notsanta.

"Just have a look out there, Dai," gasped Haemar.

Dai peered out of the side window, his dragon eyes piercing through the darkness.

"There's four of them," he reported. "There's an older one, dressed in grey, who seems to be shouting a lot. Three others, all dressed in black. They seem to be shouting, too"

The tour bus tilted to one side, and adjusted course .

"This is the final approach to The Grotto," Notsanta told them. "We'll be landing shortly, better sit down and strap yourselves in."

The Banned quickly did as they were told. The snow looked very close now, and the reindeer were clearly slowing down. With a bump, and a bounce, they were on the ice cap, and Eddie was cursing under his breath and fighting to control the skidding Sprinter. After a moment he managed to halt the wild slide and as his passengers drew breath, the jet-black Notsleigh slid past with the occupants yelling wildly, straight into an enormous mound of snow.

"I hope that they haven't damaged my Notsleigh," grumbled Notsanta, and climbed out of the tour bus. The dwarfs shivered in the sudden inrush of freezing cold air, and Haemar panicked, as Fungus turned blue instead of green.

"Quick! Someone throw something warm over Fungus!"

Dai climbed into the front seat, and Fungus, starting to freeze, slumped against him. GG was about to slam the door shut when Notsanta returned with four bedraggled looking figures.

"Get this lot in with you, then follow The Sleigh!" he ordered.

"What about you?" asked GG.

"I'm fine!"

GG slammed the door shut, Eddie turned the heater on full, and The Banned turned to look at the new arrivals.

"Hi, lads," mumbled Ned from his place at the bottom of the heap.

"Fancy meeting you here!" said Haemar.

The Grey Mage raised one hand, but Dai slid back over the seat and squashed him instead.

"I hate ter ask this," Ned managed to carry on.

"Any chance of some passes fer your gig?" blurted out the assistant assistant.

Fungus and Haemar looked at each other, with mischief in their eyes.

Haemar threw back his head, and tipped a complete can of beer down his throat. He looked at out over the happy, excited crowd, towards the center of the hall. Eddie saw his look, and waved back.

"At this point in the gig," Haemar yelled into his mic, "it would be great if you would show yer appreciation for our temporary road crew. There wasn't quite enough power here fer us tonight, so they've been taking turns in that old treadmill you've got, to keep all the stage lights going! Saving some reindeer from doing it!"

The crowd made an unidentifiable roar. Inside the treadmill,, sweaty and exhausted, The Grey Mage made a similar noise. He grabbed Ned by the arm, and was vaguely surprised that it stayed attached to the rest of Ned.

"When we get home, they are so going to regret this," he hissed.

"At least we're going to get home though, Boss. Haemar and Fungus promised, and we can trust them on that."

"What are they playing now?"

"*Shaking all over*, Boss. Nearly done now."

"Yes, I think that I am. But when we get home… Well revenge is a dish best served cold as they say."

"Just put it outside here, Boss. It'll be freezin' cold in moments."

"Shut up and jog. At least it will keep us warm."

If you liked *The Vampire Mechanic,* you can find updates and information on new releases about Fungus and The Banned on Facebook at : www.facebook.com/BannedUnderground

Or their website : www.thebannedunderground.com

If you are bored and desperate, there's the author's website

www.willmacmillanjones.com

And if you love reading, the Publisher's website:

www.redkitepublishing.net

The Banned Underground Collection: all stories are stand alone - you do not need to have seen a previous gig to enjoy any of the books.

The Amulet of Kings   (2011)

The Mystic Accountants (2012)

The Vampire Mechanic (2012)

Bass Instinct   (2013)

The SatNav of Doom   (2013)

Have Frog Will Travel   (2014)

Working Title   (2015)

A Teacher's Lot   (2015)

ABOUT THE AUTHOR

Will Macmillan Jones is a fifty something lover of blues, rock and jazz who spends his leisure time walking the hills and fells of Wales. He still peers into caves in the hope of finding a dragon to talk to: it hasn't happened yet, but it is only a matter of time....

When not procrastinating on various social media sites he writes fantasy, horror and childrens' books.

www.willmacmillanjones.com

Made in the USA
Charleston, SC
09 February 2017